Henry Peterson, Henry Peterson

Poems

Henry Peterson, Henry Peterson

Poems

ISBN/EAN: 9783743427563

Manufactured in Europe, USA, Canada, Australia, Japa

Cover: Foto ©Andreas Hilbeck / pixelio.de

Manufactured and distributed by brebook publishing software (www.brebook.com)

Henry Peterson, Henry Peterson

Poems

POEMS.

POEMS

BY

HENRY PETERSON.

———

PHILADELPHIA:
J. B. LIPPINCOTT & CO.
1863.

TO

THE MEMBERS

OF THAT

HARD WORKING. POORLY REWARDED

EDITORIAL PROFESSION,

WHO MAKE SO MANY REPUTATIONS

FOR OTHERS,

AND SO FEW FOR THEMSELVES,

THIS BOOK

IS RESPECTFULLY DEDICATED

BY

ONE OF THE FRATERNITY.

CONTENTS.

POEMS.

LYON.

Sing, bird, on green Missouri's plain,
  Thy saddest song of sorrow;
Drop tears, oh clouds, in gentlest rain
  Ye from the winds can borrow;
Breathe out, ye winds, your softest sigh,
  Weep, flowers, in dewy splendor,
For him who knew well how to die,
  But never to surrender.

Uprose serene the August sun
  Upon that day of glory;
Upcurled from musket and from gun
  The war-cloud grey and hoary.
It gathered like a funeral pall,
  Now broken and now blended,
Where rang the bugle's angry call,
  And rank with rank contended.

(9)

Four thousand men, as brave and true
　　As e'er went forth in daring,
Upon the foe that morning threw
　　The strength of their despairing.
They feared not death—men bless the field
　　That patriot soldiers die on—
Fair Freedom's cause was sword and shield,
　　And at their head was Lyon!

Their leader's troubled soul looked forth
　　From eyes of troubled brightness;
Sad soul! the burden of the North
　　Had pressed out all its lightness.
He gazed upon the unequal fight,
　　His ranks all rent and gory,
And felt the shadows close like night
　　Round his career of glory.

" General, come lead us!" loud the cry
　　From a brave band was ringing—
" Lead us, and we will stop, or die,
　　That battery's awful singing."
He spurred to where his heroes stood,
　　Twice wounded—no wound knowing—
The fire of battle in his blood
　　And on his forehead glowing.

Oh, cursed for aye that traitor's hand,
  And cursed that aim so deadly,
Which smote the bravest of the land,
  And dyed his bosom redly;—
Serene he lay while past him prest
  The battle's furious billow,
As calmly as a babe may rest
  Upon its mother's pillow.

So Lyon died! and well may flowers
  His place of burial cover,
For never had this land of ours
  A more devoted lover.
Living, his country was his bride,
  His life he gave her dying;
Life, fortune, love—he naught denied
  To her and to her sighing.

Rest, Patriot, in thy hill-side grave,
  Beside her form who bore thee!
Long may the land thou died'st to save
  Her bannered stars wave o'er thee!
Upon her history's brightest page,
  And on Fame's glowing portal,
She'll write thy grand, heroic rage,
  And grave thy name immortal!

AWAKE, MY SOUL!

Awake, my soul! nor longer pine
   In foolish, weak regret;
Go forth, and in a path divine
   Thy little griefs forget.
Take down thy sword, whose blade too long
   Hath felt corroding breath,
And battle do with hoary Wrong,
   The stern ally of Death.
               Awake, my soul!

Lo! Truth lies prostrate at the gate
   Where Falsehood reigns in might;
Corrupt are Pulpit, Bar and State,
   They will not plead her right.
Do thou, with weapons pure, the walls
   Of bloated Wrong assail,
Until her haughty rampart falls,
   As fell the idol Baal.
             Be strong, my soul!

(12)

Let robbery have its hated name,
    Liars with liars herd ;
For thee, eat not the bread of shame,
    And be thy oath thy word.
Let others crawl their crooked course,
    Or hunt like wolves by night ;
Walk thou erect, and shame, perforce,
    Their darkness with thy light.
            Be pure, my soul !

The woes of poverty allay,
    That scourge with misery rife ;
And bid wealth mend its spendthrift way,
    For what it wastes is life.
That State alone is truly free,
    Where all men may compare ;
Then favor thou that liberty,
    That gives to each his share.
            Be just, my soul !

For them that steal let there be locks,
    For idlers wrath and scorn ;
But muzzle not the mighty ox
    That treadeth out the corn.
No better and no surer right
    To earth's increase is found,
2

Than his whose arm, with brawny might,
  Hath wrung it from the ground.
              Yes, just, my soul!

Then soul, go forth, and pine no more,—
  With gloomy thoughts have done;
Jesus his cross in silence bore,
  Thy woes to His are none.
A champion be to all that bleed
  Beneath oppression's rod;
So may'st thou, in thy hour of need,
  Sweet mercy find with God.
              Go forth, my soul!

ABRA'S VISION.*

Abra Ham Lincoln, may his tribe increase,
Awoke one night—for wonders ne'er will cease—
And saw amid the gaslight in his room,
Looking as dark as the great day of doom,
A grinning negro, black, grotesque and old.
Long thoughts of war had made our Abra bold;
" What wantest thou?" he to the phantom cried.
" I wants to know, old mars'," the form replied,
" What you be gwine to do wid dis ere chile ?"
Abra Ham frowned, then said with serious smile,
" 'Tis written in Heaven, and this is my decree—
Both you and yours henceforward must be free.
My word is given.   And now, old man, depart."
But why upsprings he with a sudden start?
No more he sees a negro, black and old,
But a fair angel, with his locks of gold,
Radiant as morn, and gladsome as the spring.
" I am the soul of that soiled, earthly thing

* Readers of poetry will not require to be told that the above was
suggested by Leigh Hunt's beautiful poem of Abou Ben Adhem.

(15)

Thou saw'st but now.   Oh, man of honest heart
And steadfast purpose, thou the Letter part
Hast chosen for thyself and for thy land !
For this one deed stand thou at God's right hand !"
The angel vanished.   Abra slept no more,
But paced all night in thought his chamber floor.

Army sabre, sword of heroes,
  Glowing in my hand,
Burnest thou for shock of battle,
  Where the foemen stand?
Longest thou for wreaths immortal,
  Plucked in danger-land?

Army sabre, sword of heroes,
  Soon shall thou and I
Swoop upon the frightened valleys,
  Like the hawk from sky—
Than the hawk thy vision keener,
  Beak more sharp and dry.

Army sabre, sword of heroes,
  What if we go down,
In the battle's hour of triumph,
  Or the battle's frown!
Living, we will wear the laurel,
  Dead, the cypress crown.

2*

Army sabre, sword of heroes,
   One will mourn our fall ;
Or, if safe we come from battle,
   Proudly yield her all.
Hark ! the bugle gaily ringeth,
   Answer we its call.

MY LITTLE DAUGHTER.

I have a little daughter,
 As sweet a child as e'er
Made sunshine in a father's heart
 With her soft and shining hair;
With her hair so soft and silky,
 And her dark and wondering eye,
And her soul as pure and spotless
 As a seraph's in the sky.

I have a little daughter,
 And she cooeth like a dove
When at the sun's declining,
 I seek my home of love.
She cooeth like the stock-dove,
 And round my neck she flings
The little arms that brush away
 The day-time's cruel stings.

(19)

I have a little daughter,
    And blessings on the hour
She first came to her father's house
    As a token of God's power !
As a token of God's power
    To bless and soothe, and bind
Heart unto heart, strong unto weak,
    And man to all mankind.

I have a little daughter,
    And often prayers will rise,—
Dumb, silent prayers, but full of tears,
    To the o'erhanging skies,—
That she may never fail her part,
    In dark temptation's strife ;
And, more than all, ne'er feel a blight
    Fall from her father's life !

HOPE AND PRAY!

Hope on, though wild and dark the night,
    And not a star appear,
Thine eye shall grow more large and bright,
    Thy sight become more clear;
Soon ev'n the dark shall yield a light
    To guide thee on thy way;
For as man's day, so is his might—
    Then hope on, hope and pray!

What though misfortunes gather round,
    Like hounds that thirst for blood,
Yield not to fear, but stand thy ground,
    As ev'n dumb beasts have stood.
He conqueror is, who bravely dies,
    And leaves his foes but clay,
While all unmarred his spirit flies—
    Then hope on, hope and pray!

(21)

And though the night be dark and wild,
　　Patience that waits may see
The stars shine forth once more with mild
　　And calm effulgency.
And though the hunt be stern and long,
　　The hounds may cease to bay,
For naught than patience is more strong—
　　Then hope on, hope and pray!

AFTER THE BATTLE.

[CHANCELLORSVILLE.]

Fling out the Flag once more
   Against the Southern sky,
Its stripes all stained with gore,
   Its stars with crimson dye;
For never on our sight
   Shone heaven's auroral gleams,
As in this hour of night
   Our country's banner streams.
       Fling out the Flag once more!

Defeat may doom a cause,
   Born of disgrace and shame—
Such needs the world's applause,
   The summer heats of fame.

Our oak but stands more fast,
   The fiercer blows the storm,
For ev'n the chilling blast
   With God's own breath is warm.
      Fling out the Flag once more!

We fight no selfish fight,
   For party or for clan,
Our cause the cause of Right,
   And universal Man ;
We fight to-day that Peace
   For centuries may be ours,
With all its glad increase
   Of Freedom's fruits and flowers.
      Fling out the Flag once more!

Why Fate still seems to chide,
   It is not ours to know,
Perhaps 'mid roots of pride
   The plough must deeper go.
Faint not, faint heart, but on—
   God is above thee, still ;
Who has the Right has won,
   Even on Calvary's hill.
      Fling out the Flag once more!

Then fling the Flag once more
   Against the Southern sky,
Its stripes all stained with gore,
   Its stars with crimson dye.
For never on our sight
   Shone heaven's auroral gleams,
As in this hour of night
   Our country's banner streams.

3

FALL GENTLY, GENTLE RAIN.

Fall gently, gentle rain, nor mar
    Her quiet sleep who lieth near;
    Let no rude sound, nor thought of fear
The blissful concord jar.

Fall gently, gentle rain, nor shade
    The empurpled glory of her dream;
    Let it flow ever like a stream
In lilied banks arrayed.

Fall gently, gentle rain, and take
    The pauses of my lady's mind
    With silvery tinklings through the blind;
Till she and morning wake.

(26)

SONG.

The Foe that lured my love from me
  Is false unto his bridal vow;
Her blossoming kisses fragrantly
  Fall on a stern, averted brow;
The soft white arms, within whose fold
  An angel might contented lie,
Encircle one whose heart is cold
  To love and love's idolatry.

On her mild face I ever gaze,
  Even as she doth gaze on him,—
No glance rewards my silent praise
  From those meek orbs in heaven that swim.
And like a large and liquid star,
  She moves around her destined sun,
Sighing that still he keeps afar,
  And scorns the beauty that is won.

(27)

Oh! it were more than death, to see
   His eye return her constant light,
For still a mournful sympathy
   Preserves my soul from utter blight;
But though his smile would rend that tie,
   My last and only joy, in twain,
Yet welcome were my misery,
   If her pale cheek might bloom again.

SONG.

Oh, bid me sing no more to-night,
　My thoughts are of the morrow morn,
The shock and fury of the fight,
　The cry of hate, the glance of scorn.

To-morrow, and our eyes may be
　Blood-red with weeping bitter tears,
For forms now full of life and glee,
　May then be stiff as frozen meres.

The cry " to arms" may sound to some
　As gaily as a lover's call ;
To me it brings the silent home,
　Bereft of one, which one is all.

The shout of victory may swell
　Each proud heart with a prouder throe ;
I weep, for ah! I know too well
　The hopes that triumph hour lays low.

3*   (29)

Then bid me sing no more to-night,
  My thoughts are of the morrow morn,
The din of arms, the wavering fight,
  The bloody field in furrows torn.

THE GOLDEN SPRING.

'Tis coming over land and sea,
  The bonny Spring ;
'Tis coming swift o'er hill and lea,
  On flashing wing.
On bare, cold fields a tint of green,
In chill grey skies a softer sheen,
On high bleak hills an air less keen,
  Proclaim the coming Spring.

'Tis coming unto every land,
  A milder Day,
When war no more, with bloody hand,
  Shall bear the sway.
In many a heart a softer flow,
On many a face a milder glow,
Soft words that melt the coming blow,
  Proclaim a milder Day.

      (31)

'Tis coming to the poor man's hearth,
    A time of love,—
When justice shall be done on earth,
    As 'tis above ;
When toil shall have its fair reward,
Nor iron monsters, grim and hard,
Crush those our Saviour in his word
    Commended to our love.

'Tis coming to the rich man's door,
    In simple guise,
When Luxury shall waste no more,
    Nor Pride despise ;
But when shall mark the rich and great,
A Roman simpleness elate,
A Christian scorn of pomp and state,
    Such as become the wise.

'Tis coming soon, on rapid wing,
    This Golden Age ;
'Tis coming like the softening Spring,
    O'er Winter's rage—
Look out, look out, the skies are blue,
Even the clouds have a golden hue,
The sun of glory's breaking through,
    All hail Christ's Golden Age !

THE YOUNG FARMER'S SONG.

I have no sparkling gems, love,
    To bind around thy brow,
I cannot bid my heart to thine
    In a golden channel flow;
And didst thou ask for these, love,
    How bitter were my part,
For the only wealth my pride can boast,
    Is a true and loving heart.

A true and loving heart, love,
    I know 'tis little worth,
For men forget that hearts in Heaven,
    Are as jewels on the earth;
But still, 'tis all I have, love,
    And thou dost ask no more,
For having this, whate'er say men,
    Thou knowest I am not poor.

Thou knowest I am not poor, love,
   My hands disdain not toil,
I fight the daily fight of man
   With the stern, rebellious soil ;
And as I sow I reap, love,
   My just and equal part—
And though I have not gold or gems,
   I've a true and loving heart.

THE SOLDIER'S STORY.

Antietam's fight had ceased at night;
  We saved a State that day—
From Maryland, *our* Maryland,
  We hurled their scum of gray.

Unharmed I stood from field of blood,
  When evening's drum-beat rang;
But at my side a form of pride
  No longer marched and sang.

The gallant heart to whom no part
  Its face of danger wore,
Who sought the strife like fuller life,
  Who loved the battle's roar;

No longer sprung our ranks among,
  With dauntless eye and tone,
Kindling in each with fiery speech,
  A manhood like his own.

At burst of morn, all pierced and torn
  By murderous steel and shell,
Death-pale but warm, we found the form
  Of him we loved so well.

All pallid now the grand white brow,
  The gay cheek's ruddy dye ;
But flashed forth still the peerless will
  From the undaunted eye.

" Comrades," he said, " this night the dead
  Their ranks shall form with me ;
Above this sphere, in heights more clear,
  We'll form our company.

" Who fall in strife, their country's life,
  Freedom and man to save,
Such spirits high can never die,
  Nor rot within the grave.

" Then mourn ye not their glorious lot
  Who, losing all, all find ;
I rather mourn their fate forlorn,
  We leave this day behind.

" Ah, those we leave ! what souls will grieve
  This hour's red record o'er,—
What anxious starts, what quaking hearts,
  When a knock comes at the door !

" My father ! tell him that I fell,
  As he would have me die,
My wounds in front, in the battle's brunt,
  With my face turned to the sky.

" My mother ! say—all gently pray ;
  Some cords are hard to untwine—
That I bless her now for her loving brow,
  And her patience half divine.

" If now I stand with Death's cold hand
  In mine, and feel no fears,
It is that He has made me free
  Who heeds a mother's tears.

" One message more—comrade, bend lower,
  It is not shame, but pride—
This very year, at Christmas dear,
  I should have claimed a bride.

4

" And on my breast, in golden nest,
   All radiant you may see,
The sunny hair of one who ne'er
   Found aught but good in me.

" Tell her we part, oh, faithful heart,
   A few short years—no more ;
Her victory won, her voyage done,
   I'll meet her on the shore.

" Upon my breast that golden nest
   Leave with its sunny hair,
Perchance 't will warm this mangled form,
   Shut out from light and air.

" Mother! home! heaven! Hark—I come !"
   The gallant soul had fled.
Our colors proud made fitting shroud—
   The blue and white and red.

We dug his grave as suits the brave,
   Beneath the battle's sod ;
But well I know his soul did go
   That moment straight to God.

SONG FOR THE TIMES.*

Hark, hark, the loud drum o'er our valleys is sounding,
  The battle-flag streams like a meteor on high,
Young hearts with bright visions of glory are bounding,
  As they shout "To the Field—for the Foeman is
    nigh!"
But amid all the clamor of war's preparation,
  The still voice of Wisdom is heard from afar,
Like a pure gleam of light through a red conflagration,
  Saying, "Peace has its triumphs, far greater than
    War!"

The warrior may triumph when, o'er the loud battle,
  Is heard the fierce shout of a victory won,
For he thinks not, inflamed by the cannon's wild rattle,
  Of the mother struck down in the form of her son.
He thinks not that long years of pain must flow over,
  Before in her bosom will heal up that scar;—
But many in sorrow too late will discover
  That "Peace has its triumphs far greater than
    War!"

*The times the above was written for were not the present, and it is therefore to be taken in a general sense, and not with any partisan meaning.

Oh, in peace, 'tis in peace that all good causes flourish,
  With steady advance to Millennial day:
Men tread down their vices, while virtues that nourish,
  Fill with heavenly fragrance these temples of clay.
Arise then, ye mighty, in Wisdom's true glory,
  And cry out aloud till men hear you afar,
That it be not forgotten, 'mid strife's bloody story,
  That " Peace has its triumphs, far greater than
    War !"

THE COMING AGE.

Of all the ages that have flown since the ruddy dawn
    of time,
None seems to me so truly great, so radiant and sub-
    lime,
As that within whose twilight porch the young soul
    now may stand,
And gaze like Moses from the Mount, on a fair and
    fertile land.

Their "forty years" of doubt and strife our sires have
    wandered on,
Since first they broke the chains of rank, the bondage
    of the throne,
Still longing ever for the old, its "flesh-pots" and its
    sin,
Like Israel at Kadesh, 'mid the desert plains of Zin.

4*   (41)

But now a better day, thank God! is breaking on the
    earth,
New times are coming with the men who with the new
    had birth,
Old hearts with olden lees in vain receive the Heavens'
    new wine,
The young alone may enter in the promised Palestine.

That coming age of peace and truth, of equal rights
    and laws,
The "golden age" of Greece and Rome, our fathers'
    "good old cause,"
Which ever on the heart of man has shed a starry
    ray,
Like that which guided to the spot where the infant
    Saviour lay,—

That promised age at length has dawned—the true
    heart sees ev'n now
Its golden light illume like heaven the topmost moun-
    tain brow,
And even in the valleys deep, where vapors still lie
    curled,
Soft rainbow hues are gliding now like shapes from a
    fairer world.

But though the Morn of Hope be thus now breaking on
our sight,
Let us forget not it may fade and leave once more the
night.
Only the valor which hath won that first effulgent
ray,
May win a further progress still to the full and perfect
Day.

Then grow not weary in thy work, young soldier, who
hath cast
Thy bright glance to the Future from the darkness of
the Past;
Cease not thy stern, unsparing war with all the false
and wrong,
And as the triumph grows more sure, let thy heart grow
more strong.

And listen not but with a smile to those who weakly
fall
Before the dead ghost of the Past, and on its greatness
call;
The old time had its stars, thou know'st—what night
is there has none?
But press thou onward and rejoice—the Future hath
its sun!

"ONLY A WOMAN'S HAIR."

The day is cold and dark—the sharp sleet drives
   All pitiless upon the dreary earth ;
It is a day to make men love their wives,
   And the home comforts of the marriage hearth.

Such joys are mine, thank God !   No more my heart
   Cons sadly o'er the lessons of despair ;
As when, with shallow and self-torturing art,
   I traced these words—" Only a woman's hair !"

Only a woman's hair !   I mind me well
   When this dark tress, lit up with golden gleams,
A sunny ringlet on a girl's neck fell—
   A slender girl, with eyes like shaded streams.

I was a boy then, with a boy's bold pride—
   She younger was, but ruled me as a queen ;
Boy-love's a jest, and yet I would have died
   To shield from harm that forehead's sunny sheen.

(44)

We older grew, and curls of golden brown
　　Now made a glory round her regal head ;
Still at her feet I laid my treasures down,
　　And held them honored by her very tread.

Then glowed the hour, all other hours above,
　　When my proud queen became a woman mild,
Yielded her sceptre in the name of Love,
　　And grew in spirit like a little child.

This dark brown tress, which gleams with threads of gold,
　　I severed then in that new hour of sway ;
Soft token of my right to have and hold
　　This second self until the judgment day.

Alas, the baffled hopes of love and youth!
　　'Twas the old story, one was rich, one poor ;
They houses had and lands, we simple truth.
　　She wrote :—" Henceforth is closed my father's door ;

" Yet always shall I love you.　I have said
　　I ne'er shall wed against my father's will—
But ne'er against my own will shall I wed.
　　Have patience, sweet ! and love me, love me still!"

Oh, foolish heart of youth! that will have bliss,
   And that at once.   I answered, she was mine,
By the long years, by her first maiden kiss,
   By vows as strong as oaths, by love divine !

I would not yield my claim.   For house or field
   Of hers I cared not; but her empty hand,
Her queenly self, I could not, would not yield,
   For all the tyrant fathers in the land.

Came back her answer—mildly toned, but firm,
   With a clear ring that well my memory knew,—
What she had said, was said.   Come calm, come storm,
   To home and love alike she would be true.

Her father was no tyrant—for her sake,
   And that he loved her, he had wrung her breast.
The future years might yet all even make.
   If they did not—within the grave was rest.

How could I hope a faithful wife to find
   In one who as a daughter sadly failed ?
Of course my steps she would no longer bind—
   "Hereafter you are free," the sad lines wailed.

I heard not then that wailing—all I heard,
    All my imbittered sight that hour could see,
Was she refused to keep her plighted word,
    And coldly said, " Hereafter you are free."

It all was o'er then.   I had built on sand
    My palace beautiful, as frail as fair !
I took this soft tress coldly in my hand,
    Saying, " And this is but a woman's hair !

" Only a woman's hair ! I madly deemed
    This hair was as an angel's—would have sworn
That curls like this round Eve's fair forehead gleamed.
    Perhaps they did—for Eve made Adam mourn.

" Ah well, I'm not the first man woman-fooled—
    Nor will I be the last such shame to bear;
For few can write, before thus sadly schooled,
    On silken tress, ' Only a woman's hair !' "

       *   *   *   *   *   *   *

Madness of madness ! but it saved my life—
    While wisely good, she drifted tow'rd the dead ;
Her cheek grew thin and pale—" Some secret strife
    Is wasting her," the grave physician said.

And change of scene was tried—that constant balm
 Of breaking hearts; as if an alien sky
Could bring again the gladness and the calm
 The bosom knew when hope soared proud and high.

In vain! 'twas all in vain!   And then, one day,
 Oh day of all days brightest! came a line
That thrilled me through.   The earth, it sank away!
 Only two words were there :—" COME ! *Geraldine.*"

" Only a woman's hair !" and yet those strands
 Of paly gold, soft jet, or gleaming brown,
Hold us with coils as sure as iron bands—
 Lift us to heaven, from heaven may drag us down!

Thus on this cold, dark day, I sit and muse.
 All cold and dark without—within a shrine ;
For by the cradle where our birdie coos,
 She sits and sings, my true-love, Geraldine!

LIFE'S CHANGES.

Like a dew drop was their darling,
    Fallen from the heaven above;
Pure as aught that earth can nourish,
    Was the offspring of their love.

Year by year she grew in beauty,
    Like her spirit, pure and mild,
Till she seemed, that lovely maiden,
    Both a woman and a child.

Then a shade came o'er her features,
    And it deepened day by day;—
What has happened to thee, maiden?
    Where has fled thy spirit gay?

From her lips no answer cometh—
    See, she seeks the forest shade,
And the soft and pensive twilight—
    What has changed the lovely maid?

5

Now the cloud has swiftly vanished,
　And a clearer, holier light
Than the radiance of her childhood,
　Beams upon our raptured sight.

Yes, again she is the centre
　Of their hopes and fondest pride;
But behold there is a stranger
　Standing by their darling's side.

With a proud and lofty bearing,
　Does the daring stranger stand;
See, she looks upon him fondly;
　See! he clasps her timid hand.

"Mother," says the youth, "forgive me!
　I your daughter's heart have won:"
"Father," says the trembling maiden,
　"Father, you have gained a son."

TO ABRAHAM LINCOLN.

[SONNET AND ACROSTIC.]

A man raised up by Heaven, oh Chief! art thou!
Both bold and prudent, fitted for the hour!
Resolved to hold with iron hand the dower
And birthright of the Free, and keep thy vow!
He who ne'er bowed to kings, to thee may bow,
As unto one anointed by God's power—
Man of the People! rising as a tower,
Like Saul, among thy brethren! Oh, be now
In soul our Samuel, hearkening to the Lord,
Nor spare the cursèd Agag of our land!
Cut out that cancer with war's sure-edg'd sword!
Oh, mercifully cruel be thy hand!
Long centuries hence thy name shall shine as one
No blame can cloud—our second Washington!

STANZAS.

Father! I am weary—
I would no longer roam
Along this life-path dreary—
   Call me home.

Oh, when I was stronger,
In the early day,
I wished each hour was longer—
   Hours of play.

Then my path was lighted
By beams from kindly eyes,
Now my way's benighted—
   Sunshine flies.

Then soft words of cheering
Nerved the fainting heart,
And with sweet endearing
   Healed each smart.

Now, alone I wander,
Cheered by no joyful chime,
And melancholy ponder
       The olden time.

—

Son! is all completed
That thou wast sent to do?
Hast thou trod thy meted
       Pathway through?

Are mankind the better?
Hast thou paid thy toll?
Hast thou struck one fetter
       From the soul?

To war and toil and quicken
I sent thee into life;
Thou wilt be sorely stricken
       In the strife.

This is thy appointed
Mission from the skies;
Thou art mine anointed—
       Man arise!

5*

When through thy long labor,
Holier love shall burn
In each toward his neighbor,
    Thou shalt return.

TO ISADORA.

FROM " A CASTLE IN SPAIN."

Bend not upon me, Lady, the wild light
   Of those large lustrous eyes—already thine
   I am, thou knowest, for a power divine
To me thou hast been since that dreamy night,
When first thou cam'st before my astonished sight,
   Like a new star in heaven, with dazzling shine,
   Mad'ning me with thy beauty as with wine.
And for thy love I would dare all the might
Of mortal man : but tempt me not to scorn
   The invisible powers, honor, and truth, and faith ;
Dear Lady, make me not a thing forlorn,
   Heir to a base life and a baser death.
Tempt me no further, weak and passion-tost—
Oh turn those eyes away, or I am lost!

TO ISADORA.

FROM " A CASTLE IN SPAIN."

Tempt me no more with lip and eye,
   Lay not thy hand on mine ;
Rather than sin to gain thy love,
   I will that love resign.

The chain is breaking, Lady, fast,
   That bound my soul to thee,
Until I lived but to record
   Thy absolute decree.

My mind has yielded to thy touch
   As to a rightful sway :
So long as I believed thee true,
   To hear was to obey.

Thy witching voice, the magic power
   That lay within thine eye,
Thy glorious face, with pride of thought
   Lighted resplendently ;

Took my soul captive—led it chained—
    Left but the wild desire
That I might press those heavenly lips
    One moment, and expire.

'Tis past, that rage of love no more
    O'ermasters all my breast;
Thy own voice broke the charm, and then
    Cold reason did the rest.

What saw thy heart in mine so foul,
    So fallen and so low,
As 't were to strike my best friend down
    Because he is thy foe?

Lady, farewell—we part to meet
    No more on life's rough sea,—
Oh, would to heaven that I had died
    Before I looked on thee!

THE OLD POETS.

What, this is life! this toil from day to day,
  This wasting labor of my heart and brain,
  Not to make glad with rich poetic rain,
The barren deserts where the earth-born stray,
But on myself to forge the fatal sway
  Of worldly care, of custom, and of pain,
  That I may soar not to the heavenly plain,
Nor at its starry founts my thirst allay!
  But though this be my lot, I still can hold
  High intercourse with them, the Free of old!
And like a caged bird, that sees at morn
  Bright wings like sunbeams cleaving through the sky,
In their bold songs forget my state forlorn,
  In their strong flight my own captivity.

TO MARY.

*" For Mary hath chosen that good part which shall not be taken
away from her."*

Sweet friend and innocent, whose pure young heart
  O'erflows with love and childlike confidence,
Forgive their folly who, with worldly art,
  Oft " palter with thee in a double sense ;"
Nor mourn that thou with thy clear truthfulness,
  Thy artless questions, and most frank replies,
Thy candor's plain and unadorned excess,
  Lightest with mirth our laughter-loving eyes :
No ! let *us* rather mourn, who may have given,
  Like our first parents, purity and truth,
For knowledge which when gained has lost us heaven,
  The sunny heaven of unsuspecting youth !
Then, Mary, keep thy singleness of heart,
For thou hast truly chosen the better part.

(59)

LINES.

When the day in sadness lingers
   On the furthest verge of light,
And with slow, uncertain fingers,
   Lifts the curtain of the night;

Then come gentle thoughts and loving,
   Pleading with bewitching art,
And with them I go a-roving
   To the maiden of my heart.

Soon I feel her presence holy,
   Soon her hand is clasped in mine,
Soon I hear her whisper lowly,
   " I am thine, yes, only thine !"

What though morn be robed in sadness,
   And the noon be bathed in tears,
If the eve renew my gladness,
   And in love consume my fears ?

What were earth if Love were banished,
But a world without a sun?
What is Love when earth has vanished?
Joyful being just begun.

6

TO C. M. C.

Thou hast an old heroic name,
  And an old Roman hate
Of all that saps with fear or shame
  The bulwarks of the State.

A hatred of the mean thou hast,
  A stern hate of the vile,
Which, long as tyranny doth last,
  No art can reconcile.

Such men as thou renew our faith
  Wrong shall not last for aye;
Their very birth a promise hath
  Of a serener day.

Though often tempted, sorely tried,
  By earthly doubts and strong,
They bear right onward 'gainst the tide
  And foaming front of wrong.

(62)

Now fettered by the world's applause,
  Now by its hate set free,
They faint not, but in Freedom's cause
  Fulfill their destiny.

TO LAURA.

ON HER SIXTEENTH BIRTHDAY.

[ACROSTIC.]

Like one who stands and views a flowery scene,
All bright and glowing 'neath a sunny sky,
Unmarked the briars that mar the landscape green,
Ravished by song of birds and wind's low sigh,
A maid of sixteen summers, thou dost stand
Viewing the sunny slopes of womanhood.
Radiant indeed is that delightful land,
Oh maiden fair, unto the pure and good.
Be thine its choicest blessings, thine the way
Enameled o'er with flowers of loveliest hue,
Roving by pleasant waters all thy day.
Then at the eve, perchance a fairer view
Shall still be thine, Heaven's portal gazing through.

Full eighteen hundred years have come and gone,
And yet I live. I live and cannot die.
Strong is this pulse, and vigorous these limbs
As when that fatal morning I awoke
Joyful and glad to see the sacrifice.
" *Thou tarry till I come !*"   With what a strange
Sharp sound rang those brief words upon my ear,—
I, half incredulous and half afraid,
Unhappiest man of men, cursed with long life,
Life long as earth's, and stars that light the earth,
And orbs that feed the ever dimming stars.
And others heard that voice and scoffing said,
" O, *he* will live forever"—kinsmen and friends ;
But as the years rolled on, nor changed my form,
Nor lost its flush of youth, nor dimmed my eye,
While round me stood companions of my morn
Palsied and bent, and I within their midst
All kingly tall and with no touch of time
Or fell disease on my unwrinkled front,

6*

Began they then to whisper with white fear,
" No, he can ne'er grow old, you heard the curse!"
And men avoided me, and even my child
Grew fearful of my presence, and my wife
Was glad to die and leave me all alone.

Thus was I made a wanderer, forced to fly
From those that knew to those that knew me not—
And this has been my lot, and will be yet
My lot until the end.　Sweet friendship's ties
Have not been all unknown even to me,
And love not all a stranger, for my heart
Is as the heart of youth, and though long time
Has given it a strange calmness, yet the sight
Of a soft face still kindles in my breast
A spark of the old flame that once I knew
Among Judea's maidens.　But no spot
Could my feet find to dwell on more than for
A swift-fled season, for all saw too soon
That I was cursed, alas, and could not die.
And poisons hurt me not, nor the cold plague,
Nor fire, nor edge of sword, nor choking waves ;
For breath is not *my* life, and through my frame
Runs blood which is not blood, but like perchance
Those arteries metallic which we find
Feeding the great bulk of the undying globe.

And other men have striven to be as I,
Have sought to mix some potent draught that should
Enchant their youth, that they too ne'er might die—
Poor fools, may they ne'er find the ill they seek.

And yet the curse has been not all a curse.
God's curses cannot!   What He wills is good,
Is always good.   His blessing smiles beneath
The stern frown of a dreadful punishment
Meekly submitted to, and I have learned
To war not with my God.   In patience calm
I bow to His decree.   Until He come
I walk the earth and bear my heavy cross,
Thrice happy if its weight compare to His.
And I shall fear not to behold once more
The glance of those meek eyes, when once again
He comes in triumph 'mid the angelic host.
I shall not fear to meet those sad, calm eyes,   .
For I shall tarry till he come with hope,
And faith that waxes not nor cold nor dim,
Eternal as my youth.   For well I know
That ages yet must pass away and die,
And men grow humbler, and love poverty
Rather than wealth touched with least show of wrong,
And competence than wealth however got,
And learn to feel that no man has a right

To gather up the rich increase of earth
And hoard it for his own most selfish use,
While others famish for the bread of life,
The life of both the body and the mind—
Full well I know that this and more than this,
Must come to pass before His hour shall come.

   And therefore I with double motive toil
To fill man's heart with love.   I whisper truths
Which other men first whisper, then aloud
Bear witness to, though curse the world and smite
As once I smote—and then all men with joy,
Wakening as if from out a gloomy dream,
Cry loud " 'Tis true! 'tis true!" And thus from truth
To steeper truth I lead their spirits on
Up to the Pisgah height from which my eyes,
And all men's eyes, shall see the promised land,
In which we are to enter and to dwell
With Jesus for our king—where hate no more
Shall stir up man 'gainst man, and selfishness
Shall prompt the soul no more to wealth or power
Above its fellows ; but as brothers dear,
Sons of one common Father, we shall dwell,
And the glad earth glide unperceived and smooth
Among the orbs of heaven, and sin and pain
And my curse be no more.

SONNET.

When this hot pulse no longer madly beats
   With fierce ambition or with wild desire,
   When all is cold that now seems so afire,
And icy death has calmed life's fever heats,
Lament ye not, as the quick spirit fleets,
   For friend or brother, husband, son, or sire ;—
   Why mourn he has escaped life's burning pyre,
He so unfit to brave its fiery sleets !
Rather rejoice to think his soul no more
   Shall quiver under Time's relentless rod ;
And lay that calmly 'neath earth's grassy floor,
   Which is of kindred to the flower and sod.
And carve this line upon the grave's sad door :
   HERE LIES ANOTHER FAILURE. PARDON, GOD !

THE POWER OF BEAUTY.

Oh, mighty is the power that beauty wields
    Over the heart of wild and ardent youth;
Despotic as that born in blood-stained fields,
    And yielded to with more of zeal and truth.
    Mark its proud rule ev'n when the demon tooth
Of fierce mistrust had fixed upon its prey,
    When France her tyrants smote and felt no ruth;
Mark ye who doubt the power of Beauty's sway,
That face as Judith's fair, the avenging saint, Corday!

Borne on the car amid the vengeful mob,
    Hear how the jeer and taunt half uttered die,
When that calm cheek, and breast which knows no sob,
    And form of matchless mould beam on the eye,
    Like eve's lone star amid a stormy sky.
Oh noble one! who in kind pity leaned
    O'er sorrow's form with soft and healing sigh,
And then with steady hand struck down the fiend
Who ruled a trembling land, with soul from mercy
    weaned.

(70)

Mark how the spell of angel loveliness
 Has bound the soul of Mentz's ardent son ;
He feels not, hears not the thick crowds which press
 Around the block, beholds but that fair one
 Whose little race of life is almost run.
Her dark eye glances on the throng around,
 And rests on his—that glance has him undone.
The swift axe falls with sharp and shuddering sound—
And what cares he for life since she the tomb has found !

 And he can rest no more, but courts his fate,
 And proudly mounts the crimson guillotine ;
Views not its horrors with the glance of hate,
 But treads its planks with smiles and joyful mien.
 Oh may not we who read this tender scene,
Think they were kindred souls, destined to be
 Partners on earth, and that one glance between
Electric spark from heart to heart ?—For thee
Death was the only life, thou brave young Deputy !

 And let us not forget that noble band
 Who leagued to right the Scottish Mary's wrong,
Proud Babington with open soul and hand,
 And Titchbourne with his friendship quick and
  strong,
 Whose path of life was strewn with flowers along.

A woman's form is fettered in yon tower,
    A lovely lip now pours no more the song ;
She droops like rose torn from its native bower,—
What, are they gallant men, and do they fear death's
    hour !

Yes, ever thus since time his race began,
    The heart of youth has bowed to beauty's spell,
The only bondage that becomes a man,
    The only tyrant he may ne'er repel.
    Lightly upon the soul the fetters dwell,
Until we fain would wander from the throne,
    But then they bind at every step, and tell
Their mighty strength by the sad, smothered moan,
Till we repenting turn, and for our sin atone.

THE EXILE'S ADDRESS TO AMERICA.

[AN EXTRACT.]

Land of my choice! thou art a fitting dwelling
  For the true-hearted, for the bold and free ;
Thy thousand tongues are eloquently telling
  That thou the exile's home shalt ever be.
  When thy great rivers come, the mighty sea
Flings wide the doors into his council hall;
  Thy lakes rush grandly on, and bend the knee,
And shout their Maker's praise ; and who can fall
Before his fellow man, when they on God thus call !

Aye, nature here proclaims in grandest tones
  The glory of her Author.   Higher and higher
Tower up the mountains, vast, cloud-curtained
    thrones
  For the Unseen to rest on.   Waves of fire
  Roll o'er the boundless prairie—nigher and nigher
Dashes their sparkling spray. Seek'st thou the
    shore,

   7   (73`

Proud man, with orders decked ? Thy funeral pyre
Is kindled. What avails thy golden store ?
The poorest serf will burn, prove now that thou art
  more.

Such are the scenes around them—what are they
  Who dwell in such a vast, Titanic home ?
A rough-hewn race, bear-cubs just brought to day,
  And not yet shaped—restless and wild they roam,
  Borne to and fro like ocean's storm-tossed foam,
By every wave of doctrine—no stray thought
  But here will find a sphere in which to loom
Through vapory space, until it seems heaven
  wrought ;
But soon they grasp the prize, and find their treasure
  naught.

A giant here was born. Yet in his spring,
  His earthly nature first comes forth in pride.
He loves to show his body's strength, to fling
  The rocks on high which bar his manly stride,
  On the black steed whose breath is flame to ride,
To turn the rivers from their olden path,
  Through upper air 'mid cloud and storm to glide,
And tame the lightning's fierce, destructive wrath,
Aye, in such things as yet, his young soul pleasure hath.

The time shall come when, his strong powers unfold-
    ding,
  He shall speak out unto his fellow man,
With all that's holy sweet communion holding,
  Careless of lordly frown or priestly ban.
  The kindling coals of truth his breath shall fan,
And beacon fires shall blaze from every height;
  And like an angel he shall lead the van
Of thronging millions battling for the right,
And then shall be laid low each proud oppressor's
    might.

Aye, he shall yet arise, and be a mouth
  To this great western world—to trumpet forth
From sea to sea, from north to farthest south,
  A new evangel to the groaning earth.
  God speed the hour when every humble hearth
Blooming and happy faces shall surround,
  Refined by knowledge, dignified by worth;
When Plenty's horn shall everywhere be found,
And Freedom's glorious form the only monarch
    crowned!

ISABEL.

Upon the cold, cold bier thy kindred laid thee,
      Isabel!
In white, pure white, young, trembling hands arrayed
 thee,
      Isabel!
As to a bridal, thrilling voices bade me,
They led me there, I knew not that they led me
    Unto thy darkened chamber, Isabel!

I gazed upon that face so coldly blooming,
      Isabel!
Upon that cheek which glowed not at my coming,
      Isabel!
Those pallid lips which parted not to bless me,
Those snowy arms which oped not to caress me,
    Those eyes, closed, closed forever, Isabel!
      (76)

I thought not of the hour, the hour I won thee,
      Isabel!
I thought not of the good thy love had done me,
      Isabel!
One feeling filled my soul, one feeling only,
That thou wert dead, and I forever lonely,
    With nothing left to live for, Isabel!

Then rose an aged man, by age unfrozen,
      Isabel!
"She lies not there," he said, "the early chosen,
      Isabel!
Those pallid lips which parted not to bless thee,
Those snowy arms which oped not to caress thee,
    She would not thus, thy own, thy Isabel!

"She has not left thee, still she stands beside thee,
      Isabel!
Still from the tempter shall her spirit guide thee,
      Isabel!
Still shall her presence comfort thee at even,
Still shall ye wander 'neath the starry heaven,
    Still shall she be thy own, thy Isabel!"

7*

And I am calm now, calm, for thou art nigh me,
                              Isabel!
In peril's hour thou movest slowly by me,
                              Isabel!
Whene'er I seek the good, the true, the holy,
Whene'er I shun the heartless haunts of folly,
          I feel thou still art with me, Isabel!

LIFE.

1.

Our life is but a bubble tost,
Now here, now there, now found now lost,
    Upon a stormy wave.
It glows perhaps with iris hues,
But like the light the lost one woos,
    They mock us to the grave.
Friendship is but another name
    For selfishness and pride ;
And love burns with unholy flame,
    Before the maid is bride.
      Now hither, now thither,
        In fruitless chase we stray,
        Our found joy a child's toy,
        Broken and thrown away.

(79)

2.

A moment more, and where is life ?
Burst by the angry waves of strife,
    It mixes with the sea.
Our brother sinks beneath the wave,
And this, his spirit's hopeless grave,
    We call "the Life to be."
His separate being is no more,
    Be he not tossed again,
To float a moment as before,
    Then mingle with the main.
        The body's fall thus merges all
        Into a mighty whole ;
        Our separate lot is all forgot
        In nature's heaving soul.

SECOND VOICE.

1.

Our life is like a twinkling star,
Seen in the depths of blue afar,
    Just visible to sight ;
Gladly along its path it goes,
And with a brighter radiance glows,
    As darker grows the night.
Friendship is sunshine freely given
    To warm the fainting soul,

And love is holy fire from heaven,
  Such as Prometheus stole.
    It nerves us, preserves us
      From every deed of shame :
    The storm blast and rain fast
      But feed its rising flame.

2.

And death is but the clad-in-mail,
Who with his spear uplifts the veil
  That dims the spirit's view ;
And life is then a glorious sun,
That like a god his race doth run,
  Where night can ne'er pursue.
Attended by a sister star,
  With softer, holier light,
Nor time nor space uprears a bar
  To their eternal flight.
    And loudly and proudly
      Their song of praise they sing,
    To Him who the heavens knew,
      Ere Time had plumed his wing.

"WILL'S ROCK."

Few days that I have passed on earth,
   Few hours of those where joy has smiled,
By running stream, or social hearth,
   In town, or forest wild,

Have left such rapture in my breast,
   Such trails as of a heavenly dream,
As one soft summer day I passed
   By Brandywine's bright stream.

For friends were there, the kind and true,
   Fair youthful friends, and good as fair ;
And overhead a sky of blue,
   And round me the pure air.

And far below the river ran ;
   And far below the cultured plain
Was smiling with the abodes where man
   His Eden rears again.

And one was near whose feet with mine
　　Along that stream had often trod,
When young love made its banks divine,
　　And walked earth like a god.

Along the river paths we strayed,
　　And o'er the rough and wooded hill,
And then our grassy couch we made
　　Upon its summit still.

With lightsome toil we reared our tent,
　　We held sweet converse, free from art;
Love hovered round where'er we went,
　　And Peace was in each heart.

And when we homeward turned again,
　　As day drew near its welcome close,
Our sun of joy set free from stain,
　　As in the morn it rose.

THE VISION.

A FRAGMENT.

In the mid hour of night, when earthly thoughts,
Those fetters of the soul, had lost their power,
And slumbered as if dead, with lightsome spring
My joyful spirit glided from its chains,
And sought with rapid wing the upper sky.
There for a time I bathed in beams that flowed
Fresh from the throne of God, and cleansed my soul
From the pollutions of its earthly state.
At length accustomed to the heavenly light,
With joy I gazed around me.   Angel forms,
Unseen at first, with spiritual eyes,
Full of deep meaning and celestial love,
Were gazing on my face, as earnestly
As a young mother on her new-born child. ,
With tones as soft as those which memory hears
In the green vale where flows our youthful love
Like a deep river tunefully along,
They welcomed me to heaven.   With holy joy

They said, they saw a star, like a bright dart,
Shoot from its crystal gate, (for stars are naught
But angel watchers of the gates of bliss,)
And hasten down to guide my soul above
To stay with them forever.   But again
They looked, and saw the body only slept;
Again to wake, again to prove its power
Over the soul, subjected for a time
In heavenly wisdom, like the Man of Uz,
To the dominion of the evil one.

The body only slept; I might not long
Delay in those glad realms—and therefore came
Two bright celestials, and with winning smile
Bade me my thoughts engage in noting well
My future home of bliss, that in the hours
Which come to all, of sorrow and of pain,
Hours when men grow aweary of the earth,
I might be nerved to endure them, nor repine
At what my fate ordained.   With them I trod
Through many a flowery path, and felt the joy
Of birds and winds and gently flowing streams.
Yes, *felt* the joy, for, not as on the earth,
Where perfect sympathy was never known,
We entered in the soul of all that was,
And felt enjoyment equal to its own.

8

Our joy was never there another's pain,
Our pain could never be another's joy.
As one increases in celestial strength,
And greater capabilities of bliss,
So all increase in strength and happiness.
No mortal man could tell the whole I saw,
No earthly tongue express the joy I felt,
Nor earthly heart conceive the bliss divine.
It is not lawful for my eager lips
To utter that which angels breathe in heaven.
In your blind wisdom did I tell you all,
You would but mock at me.   Then let it rest
Like a bright sunbeam in my heart of hearts,
Not to flash forth until the judgment day.

But I may tell of that which I have seen
Of man's triumphant fortunes.   When with sad
And lingering look on all the liquid joys,
Thus flowing in and mingling with each other,
I turned me to depart, I saw below,
Stretched like infinity before my eyes,
A sight of wondrous woe and power and beauty.
The world, not the corporeal only, but its life,
Which is the incorporeal and the real,
The past, the present, and the future time,
In body, soul and spirit 'neath me lay.

Oh for a pen like his who found fit words
To veil from mortal sight the heavenly rays
Transfixed in the divine Apocalypse,
And yet left bright what man might know and live!
Oh for a vision touched by heavenly hand,
Like what enabled me to view the course
Of ages all unrolled, that you might see
What I have seen, but cannot fully tell.
Oh for a faith like that which prompted him
Whose only son upon the altar lay,
That you might bind the fiend whom men call Gain,
And raise at heaven's command the ready knife,
That all may see that he is not your God.

For Mammon is the only evil power,
The only Idol of rebellious man,
That is entirely earthy.   All the rest
Are the descendants of those mortal maids,
For whom the sons of God forgot their place
In the bright realms above ; renouncing their
Eternity of bliss for the warm arms
And passionate embrace of human love.
And thus their children, sinful though they be,
For good can never from the unnatural come,
Oft show some traces in their low estate
Of a pure nature not entirely lost.

But Mammon is the child of Earth alone.
Defying God when our first parents fell,
She sought in fearful pride her inmost caves,
And gloated o'er the treasures by whose aid
She hoped to conquer the Eternal One.
Weary at length with her obscure abode
And solitary state, and daring not
To venture where the sound of lute-like leaves,
Touched by the fingers of the maiden Spring,
And ever happy songs, beguile the good
From their sad loneliness, she fed the hope
That one might spring perhaps from her own side
To comfort her in her dull solitudes.
The strong desire at length, as God so willed,
Produced fulfilment, and ere long a child
Crept stealthily the floors of her dark caves.
Sullen he was from very infancy,
Sullen and fierce, save when his little hands
Would grasp unlooked-for some rich wedge of gold
Or there dull diamond, which unknowing why
He would conceal, creeping with cautious eye
But careless aspect towards a secret nook
Where he could hide secure his precious prize.
For miles his boyish steps would often trace
Some rich, meandering vein of virgin gold,
And wish the time had come when with man's strength

He might enslave these creatures of the mine.
Thus as he grew in years he grew in all
That even unto the vile is odious.
His mother first would by her lonely side
Have kept the boy, but soon his face became
A loathing ev'n to her ; for she had marked
His gaze oft resting on her queenly crown,
Studded with brilliant stones unknown to man,
Whose starry rays need not the quickening power
Of sun or moon to call them into life.
She therefore shunned his presence, and a fear
Would often press with cold and heavy hand
Upon her heart, when he would cross her path
Where a wild river flung its ebon length,
As if impelled by some resistless power,
Moaning aud writhing down the soundless depths
Of the unfathomed globe.   Well might she fear,
That hapless mother ! she had proudly mocked
The eternal voice that called her into life,
And now the wicked child of her own womb,
In silent thought against his mother's breast
Oft lifted up the matricidal hand.
Once when in saddest thought she stood upon
The jagged rocks that rear their horrid heads
Where madly howls the miserable stream,
Whose wretched fortune I could almost mourn,
      8*

She felt a strange desire to gaze within
That fearful gulf, into whose gloomy depths
The river flowed with a perpetual moan
Forever and forever.   Treading slow
She stepped from rock to rock, against which roared
Madly the foaming flood, at often times
Veiling her dizzy eyes with trembling hand,
From the wild whirling waters, till at length
Upon the utmost verge of the abyss
She in her weakness stood.   She summoned strength,
And leaned with terror o'er the awful depths
Of that infernal gulf.   No sound was there
Of water dashing on the rocks below ;
Naught but the moaning of the waves above,
And the swift rushing of the falling stream,
Met her attentive ear.   With straining eyes
She sought to pierce the blackness, but in vain ;
Until at length it took demoniac shapes,
And beckoned her to come.   She would have screamed,
But could not—nor withdraw her frightened gaze
From the dark phantoms of that hideous gulf.
With a strong will she oft would slowly raise
Her stiffened eyes, but the swift-falling stream
Would drag them down again.   At length she nerved
Her weary soul, and summoned all her strength
For the last, struggling effort of despair.

With a loud shriek she broke the hellish charm,
And tore her eyes from the infernal depths.
Short victory! for her limbs had lost their power,
And ever and anon her spell-bound sight
Would wander downward with a dread desire
To meet those serpent eyes—she cannot move—
She turned her head—oh, welcome, welcome sight!
There comes her son, a loathing now no more.
She cries aloud, "Help, help, thy mother dies!"
He answers not, but springs from rock to rock
Like the wild chamois. He is by her side,—
A moment longer, and he were too late;
For see she totters on the narrow brink.
"Give me thy hand," she moans, with piteous glance.
He reaches forth his hand, and plucks the crown
From her imperial head, then slowly turns,
And leaves her to her fate. The fiendish act
For a short moment nerved the mother's soul,
And as he partly turned, he started back
From the indignant glance that pierced him through;
Then overcome she shrieked, and headlong plunged
Into that horrid gulf, that gate of Hell.
Her further fate, how far she fell, how long,
It matters not, my pen too long delayed
Already, from the account of what I saw

When from that height celestial I gazed down
With more than mortal vision.   Nor had I
Thus turned aside for aught of trifling worth.
But in this land by God so highly blessed,
Mammon hath many worshippers ; alas!
This meanest of false gods, who hugs his gold,
Begrudging ev'n its sacrifice to build
A temple to himself, is worshipped here
Even by youth and beauty.   Yet is he
No generous master to the servile crowd
That throng around his vile, worm-eaten throne.
Moloch, infernal king! besmeared with blood,
Will shower elate upon the horrid crew
That follow where his crimson footsteps lead,
His hateful gifts of rapine and of murder :
For them upon the gory battle-field
He spreads a banquet worthy of a fiend.
There they may quaff from early morn till eve,
From the rich vein, until they're drunk with blood,
While birds obscene fan them with wanton wing,
And shrieks and groans are their inspiring songs.
Fall down and worship him, and these are yours.
But Mammon is a miser even to those
Who are his humblest slaves.   He answers not
When importuned for gold, or with a whine

Says he is poor, too poor! and feeds his crowd
Of parasites on garbage from the sewers.
And yet man, poor, infatuated man,
Made in God's image, will bow down before
This meanest of the dark, rebellious powers,
In miserable worship.

     But I turn
From this unhappy theme, to touch with joy
The harp of inspiration—to unfold
Before your mental vision what I saw,
When from my heavenly height I gazed on all
That ever was, or is, or is to be,
Upon this rolling globe. Presumptuous hope!
Who can reveal in words the infinite?
That scene, before my spiritual eye
As vivid as the lightning, darts away
When I would fetter it in earthly sounds.
Censure me not then if I sadly fail
In this my task divine, and judge me not
By the cold rules of reason, for the soul
Poetic and prophetic is a rule
Unto itself, and may no more be bound
Than the Aurora's soft celestial gleams.
Like it then may I hope to lighten up

The dusky realms of what to man is night,
Not with a radiance like the summer sun,
Beneath whose brilliant dart the darkness dies,
But with continuous streams of fitful light,
Behind whose rosy veil the meek-eyed stars,
Faith, Hope, and Charity, gaze sweetly down.

It was the morning of the seventh day,
The sabbath of creation, and the earth
From all her dewy flowers and fragrant herbs,
Breathed forth a prayer of thankfulness to Him
Who called them into life. The sky-lark winged
With the first blush of morn his rapid flight
Into the blue profound, and poured his heart,
So clear and joyous, like a crystal stream,
On the sustaining air. Panting with bliss,
The songsters of the grove in leafy nooks
Trilled their inspiring notes, until they seemed
Embodied music ; and the nightingale,
Forgetting in his joy that day was come,
Flung out in glory his surpassing strain,
And led the heavenly choir. The little brooks
In joyous tinklings told their thankfulness ;
And mighty ocean with his rushing roar,
Like a vast organ, pealed aloud in praise.

But still more grateful to the Father's ear
Rose the deep voice of Adam, as in prayer
He bowed himself before the Eternal Throne.
He had come forth from the embowering shade,
With her whom God had given him when he told
Of his sad loneliness, and as he marked
The beauty of the earth, and heard the birds
Breathe forth the deep praise of their passionate hearts,
And looked on her his bride, surpassing all
In her young loveliness, he knelt him down,
O'ercome with grateful thought, and thanked the Lord
For his unnumbered gifts.   His youthful bride
For a brief moment stood irresolute,—
A moment stood, as doubtful how to act,—
And then beside him knelt, her gentle arm
Around him softly thrown, while the big tears,
Unknowing why they flowed, upon the grass
In gentle droppings fell.   From thence, 'tis said,
The modest violets sprung.   The few short words
Their hearts had prompted said, they from the ground
In humbleness arose.   Beautiful pair !
And pure as beautiful ! no sinful thought
Had dimmed the innocent lustre of the eye,
Nor marred the tuneful cadence of the voice,
Nor paled the hollow cheek.   Both beautiful,

And yet how different in grace of form,
In countenance and air.   His beauty was
That of the ruddy even, hers was like
The fair and gentle morn.   The ebon hair,
Like a dark, severed stream, in parted waves
From his high brow flowed curling. ·Large black eyes,
Emblems of strength, and passion, which is strength
In chaos————

LINES.

Great Power of Love ! on our own strength relying,
  We sink beneath the vapory shade of earth,
Till sorrow-stricken, weary, sad and sighing,
  We mourn the hour which gave the spirit birth.

With hopeless heart—yes, hopeless, though believing—
  We turn to Thee for heavenly warmth and rest,
As a boy pilgrim, from the world's deceiving,
  Turneth disheartened to his mother's breast.

Thou breathest in our souls sweet consolation,
  Thou heal'st the wounded heart with strains of love,
And whisperest of a glorious salvation,
  And bright perfection, in a world above.

Again we turn and arm us for life's battle,
  Again we tread our two-fold way along;
The body where sin's volley'd thunders rattle,
  The spirit in the blessed land of song.

9   (97)

LAUREL HILL.

1.

Sweet Laurel Hill! how can I pass thee by,
　　Nor pour my tribute on thy quiet air!
Though broken be my verse as mourner's sigh,
　　Yet may it claim alike the merit rare
　　Of springing from the heart; for oft when care
Has twined too closely round me, have I trod
　　Among thy graves, and felt I might not wear
Guiltless the chains of earth, nor kiss its rod—
"For life is but a span," was whispered from the sod.

2.

The young and innocent have here been laid
　　Beneath the flowering vine and sculptured stone,
To sleep until the voice of Him who made,
　　Shall rouse them from their rest with trumpet-tone.
　　Sweet calm is theirs.　Alas, the mother's moan,
And trembling frame, have told her stifled woe,
　　Who leaves this spot henceforth to tread alone
The path of life, and feel she may not know
Again the pressing lip, and "Mother," murmured low.

(98)

3.

And to these shades in all her opening bloom,
    The youth has borne his fair and happy bride.
Oh! why did not the messenger of doom
    Bid him prepare to lie down by her side?
    As they have lived in love, why not have died
Each in the other's arms?   Most Holy Power!
    It seemèd good to Thee thus in the pride
Of youthful bliss to pluck this beauteous flower—
Oh! give to him the strength he needs in such an hour!

4.

Affection here has reared the marble pile,
    And planted the white rose and evergreen,
And graven on the stone in varied style
    The names of those who may no more be seen.
    The hoary sire, and girl of gay sixteen,
And he who steps from cradle to the grave,
    Nor knows there is a busy life between,
All sink with tears beneath oblivion's wave—
For some will mourn the death ev'n of the vilest knave.

5.

Think not there lives the man so wholly lost
    To all the kindly feelings of the soul,
That when his bark of life, long tempest-tossed,

At length goes down, and waves above it roll,
    No hand for him a mournful chime will toll,
To tell the world the story of his fate.
    A mother lives his kindness to extol,
A widow mourns a home left desolate,—
For never lived the heart that could not find its mate.

6.

Far toward the west there stands a monument,
    Whose hapless tale the hearer can but mourn.
A wife from a fond husband has been rent,
    Six children from their father have been torn ;
    And, left to toil through life, bereft, forlorn,
He raised this tribute to their memory—
    A marble base, now weather-brown and worn,
Upholds a broken column, meant to be
An emblem of the ruin wrought, oh Death, by thee !

7.

Upon one side of the square base are told
    The names and ages of his household band,
Laid side by side, like lambs within the fold :
    And on another the sad sculptor's hand
    Has carved a full blown rose, like those the bland

Air from the sunny south loves to caress;
    And on the branch, by softest breezes fanned,
Six buds uplift their infant loveliness—
And fancy sees soft eyes which make us turn and bless.

8.

For all were cut off in their early day,
    But one had seen the seventh summer's sun,
They fell before the frost like flowers in May,
    And as their stems were severed, one by one,
The ties which bind to earth were all undone
Within the mother's breast—she might not stay,
    When those she loved the grave's cold kiss had won.
She wandered 'mid their scenes of merry play,
And heard sweet voices cry,—"Dear Mother, come
    away!"

9.

As mournful is the tale this statue tells
    Of her, the wanderer from the sunny Rhine,
Who sought an exile's home where Freedom dwells,
    With him who fled from ruthless Constantine.
Her sweet, sad German face, as o'er a shrine,
Bends o'er her infant cherubs, with that love
    Than aught on earth more precious and divine.
    13*

A holy calm as from the heaven above,
Seems resting on the spot, and bids us gently move.*

10.

And one sleeps here who, when the cloud of war
 Hung heavy with defeat, disgrace and shame,
When " Hull's surrender" left a crimson scar,
 That on the nation's forehead burned like flame,
 Made HULL once more a grand, heroic name,
And cooled men's brows with breezes from the sea.
 Thou wast of those whose thunders first did tame
The ancient Tyrant of the waters free,
Sharing with all mankind the fruits of victory !

11.

Thy country o'er thy dust no column rears,
 She mourns thee not save with her poets' sighs,
Thy simple monument embalms no tears
 Shed for a hero by a people's eyes.
 This tomb, this starry flag that on it lies,

* Helena Schaaf—wife of Henry Dmochowski Saunders—born in Neustadt-on-the-Rhine, May 24, 1823, died in Philadelphia, July 8, 1857. The statue is in a beautiful situation, and faces down the river. An inscription in Latin, informs the reader that the husband is a Polish exile, and the effigy the work of his own hand.

This eagle clutching bold the deadly ball,

Tell but of him a woman's heart did prize,

Tell but of her who lost in him her all,

And for whose "private" worth her tear-drops proudly
fall.*

12.

Farther below a granite column towers,

Raised to the memory of Erin's son,†

Who knelt at freedom's shrine in those dark hours,

When there to kneel was fearful risk to run.

Praise to his name! the battle-field was won,

And long he lived to mark a goodly tree,

Spreading its branches to the air and sun.

Oh! would to God that all beneath were free!

May *his* tomb need no hand of " Old Mortality!"‡

---

* It was while the country was excited to the uttermost by mingled
rage and shame at the disgraceful surrender of General *William* Hull,
at Detroit, in August, 1812, that the news came of the capture of the
English frigate Guerriere, Captain Dacres, by the Constitution, com-
manded by Captain *Isaac* Hull. His tomb bears the following inscription:—"In affectionate devotion to the private virtues of Isaac Hull,
his widow has erected this monument."

† Charles Thomson. First, and long the confidential secretary of
the Continental Congress. Born in Ireland, November, 1729, died in
Philadelphia, August 16, 1824, in his *ninety-fifth* year.

‡ A fine group of statuary, carved in sandstone by the Scottish
sculptor Thom, represents Walter Scott listening to the stories of
"Old Mortality."

13.

For here is also seen that gray-haired man,
 His form upraised above the mossy stone,
Telling their fate whom the unsparing ban
  Of priestly power that swayed a tyrant's throne,
  Had forced to speak with startling musket-tone,
And far from home in shaded glens to lurk,
  Till Bothwell from its slain sent up a moan
For vanquished faith and persecuted Kirk—
Ah! they that sleep beneath could tell of that day's work.

14.

And standing near with grave and thoughtful eye,
 Listens the bard of Scotia's gifted land,
Whose barren mountains and whose wintry sky,
  Flushed with romance beneath the glowing hand
  Which made her annals beautiful and grand;
He hears of him who knew no idle fear,
  Bold Burley, and his dauntless peasant band,
And nobler Morton, with his soul sincere,—
While the "White Pony" lends a grave, attentive ear.

15.

Unhappy Neal! how little they do know
 Of that mysterious thing, the human heart,
Who deem that 'neath its bright and mirthful flow,

No grief e'er lurks with sad, embittered dart.

Thine was the jester's gay, fantastic part,

E'en 'mid the tortures of disease and care;

But ever informed with wisdom was thy art.

" Alas, poor Yorick !" in a milder air

May'st thou with joy unlearn the lessons of despair.

16.

Greater than thou was he whose tomb away

In solitude, so dear to dreamer's soul,

My wandering footsteps found unsought one day,

Upon the ranges of the wooded knoll.

Afar I saw the calm, broad river roll,

Like a great life its destined pathway down,

And through green leaves the sun's keen dia-
monds stole,

Gemming the rugged marble with a crown.

Whose lonely grave is this ?   The grave of BROCKDEN
BROWN !*

---

* Charles Brockden Brown, born in Philadelphia, January 17, 1771, died February 22, 1810, aged thirty-nine years. Griswold, in his " Prose Writers of America," says :—" Brown was the first American who chose literature as a profession, and the first to leave enduring monuments of genius in the fields of the imagination. * * * He was a man of unquestionable genius and a true scholar. His works are original, powerful and peculiar, and with all their faults, will continue to be read by educated and thoughtful men." His principal works are Wieland, Ormond, Arthur Mervyn, Edgar Huntley and Clara Howard.

17.

Ah, child of genius, and of sorrow, too,
   How my young heart thrilled 'neath thy tragic
      page!
First in this Western land the Muse to woo,
   And with feigned woes life's bitter griefs assuage.
   These glorious hills saw Wieland's maniac rage,
They heard that voice he madly deemed from
      Heaven—
   Innocent murderer! deluded sage!
And ours the streets young Arthur trod at even,
Dark, desolate, and still—struck by the Plague's cold
      levin.

18.

They live ev'n yet, those children of thy mind—
   And can it be then, Brown, that thou art dead?
That thou art gone, and left no trace behind,
   Save what now moulders in this darksome bed?
   That soul of fire, which lit with lurid red
The ebon clouds of circumstance and crime,
   Has it, a meteor light, but burned and fled?
Or dwell'st thou now within some fairer clime,
Oh spirit too finely framed for earth and care and
      time?

19.

No answer cometh from this quiet grave,
  No word but Peace is breathing from thy mould;
" Peace," say the shadows as they softly wave,
  " Lie down and sleep within this peaceful fold."
  No more than Peace! earth's lesson soon is
    told.
Only within the soul itself a cry
  Comes struggling forth, as man and nature old,
And witness bears that it shall never die,
But live and love, or hate, through all eternity.

20.

He well may trust that voice whose children fair,
  And friends beloved, were laid this sod beneath;
Oh, visions of soft eyes and sunny hair,
  Ye could not vanish like a passing breath!
  Thou couldst not take them utterly, oh Death!
Still must they live upon some brighter shore,
  Still with gay flowers their fair young foreheads
    wreathe,
Still with warm hearts the great Supreme adore,
Growing in grace and strength and beauty evermore!

21.

Oh! wise are they who beautify the tomb,
  And wean us from our foolish, childish dread,

Who charm from off the soul its robe of gloom,
    When o'er the grave our footsteps lightly tread.
    Ah! well I know that soon this fevered head,
Beneath thy surface, oh, thou Earth! must lie,
    But half the bitterness of death is fled,
To think that o'er my grave the gentle sigh
Will sometimes softly come, from loved ones bending
    nigh.

WORDS.

War to the knife,
    And the knife to the hilt;
Wave it in air,
    With the red blood gilt;
Fling it aloft,
    Till it stick in the sky;
There let it stick
    Till we conquer or die!

THIRST NOT FOR IOWA.*

Though tales may come, as came of old,
    Of gardens in the west,
Where man may dwell with ease and gold
    And love supremely blest;
Yet earth is earth, where'er it be,
    And work is never play,
And who will have sweet minstrelsy,
    He must the piper pay.

      And so my lads and lasses,
        My lads and lasses gay,
      Drink still from your old glasses,
        Nor thirst for Iowa.

In distant view our eyes we turn
    To the horizon's rim,
Heaven seems so near the earth, we burn
    To hear the angelic hymn;
But as all ardor we advance,
    We find the heavens still far,
And own that space, like young romance,
    Paints things not as they are.

* Written upon the failure of a projected emigration scheme.

13   (109)

Thus from man's cradle to his tomb,
   Hope's brightest hour's to-morrow,
The future shineth through the gloom
   That clouds his heart with sorrow;
But, comes the future, 'tis to-day,
   The same old weary Present;—
And could we grasp the moon, I lay
   'Twould prove some dull tin crescent.

   And so my lads and lasses,
     My lads and lasses gay,
   Drink still from your old glasses,
     Nor thirst for Iowa.

Oft when I stand among the selfish throng
  Who crowd the busy avenues of trade,
Upon my spirit flutters many a song,
  That in my heart its downy nest has made ;
And then I grieve that I to thee, sweet bird,
  May not devote my every thought, my all,
And wander where ennobling sounds are heard,
  By the wild wood and tuneful waterfall.
But soon I banish such despondency,
  And pray for strength to walk within that way
That has in wisdom been appointed me,—
  For well I know that He whom worlds obey,
If it be right my hopeful bark will guide
Where Poesy's enchanting waters glide.

(111)

AFTER A LECTURE.

I loved to hear him best who told
    The fate of the great Montrose;
How on the bloody block he died,
    Victorious o'er his foes.

For of all the men who light the gloom
    Of England's troubled age,
Few seem so free from littleness,
    So full of noble rage.

And he who wreathes another leaf
    Around the hero's head,
Or freshens with his tears the grass
    Above the glorious dead;

Who keeps alive in common men,
    Honor's soon smothered flame,
Himself may lead a hero's life,
    And win a deathless name.

MEMORY.

When sorrows o'er the bosom steal,
  Like clouds that hide the sunny ray,
And with their gloomy robe conceal
  The cheerful beauty of the day;
  And I could almost madly pray
For the dread quiet of the grave ;
  Kind Memory like an angel flies,
My soul from dark despair to save,
  And bids it from the earth arise,
And stand erect like franchised slave.
  Within her train come happy hours
That answered to my childhood's call,
  Around her brow are wreathed the flowers
  That boyhood plucked in pleasure's bowers,
And from her sweet lips gently fall
  The thrilling love-tones on my heart;
And as I stand entranced a voice
Within me cries, " Rejoice ! Rejoice !"
  My sorrows fly—a sunny dart
Has pierced them through, and hope once more
Gilds all my feelings as before.

PATIENCE.

Possess thyself in patience, soul, nor strive
   To do great works thou hast no call to touch ;
   Even he who doeth little doeth much,
If he unvexed but keep his heart alive,
Ready for some proud day of sacrifice.
   We should not move but at the Master's call.
   The soldier who with ill-timed rage doth fall
Upon the enemy's front, shows not less vice
Than he who shuns the combat, when the roll
   Of the great drums, and all the noise of war,
Blend with the stern cry, Forward ! and the whole
   Dark mass sweeps on, while shakes the earth afar.
Be patient then and tranquil, oh my soul!
   Rashness the best and purest cause may mar.

CORA.

Houris in the heaven above,
Equal ye my ladye-love?
Spirits of the summer air,
Have ye shapes that are as fair?
Daughters of the ocean king,
With the gold-fish wandering,
Do your eyes a lovelier view
In the gorgeous depths of blue?

Hers is not a form of light,
Flashing past the raptured sight,
Or with gentle motion stealing
From the heart each stormy feeling;
But a form where grace you see
Blended with sweet dignity,
Moving by you like a queen,
With a soft yet noble mien.

Features are not hers that tell
Mirth rings there like merry bell;
Unlike those of jest and folly,
Or affected melancholy;

But are those which answer well
To her soul's bewitching spell,
Lighting with enthusiast feeling,
Blushing then at the revealing.

Eyes there are which sparkle mirth,
Like a sunlit stream of earth,
Or with scorn can lightning flash
From beneath the cloudy lash;
But her glances seem to burn,
When on you they proudly turn,
Piercing to the heart like steel,
Wounding only though to heal.

But why tell of outward grace,
Queenly form, or speaking face,
Noble forehead, broad and high,
Or a bosom burning eye?
Let me sing of mental charms,
Cradled in her beauty's arms,
Thoughts of fire which blazing dart,
Lighting up the kindred heart.

Words which flash as wild they run,
Witty speech, or sportive pun,
Or the merry look so droll,
Come not from her ardent soul.

But from out her bosom flow
Thoughts that with warm feeling glow,
Which, half-uttered, she would fain
Prison in her heart again.

But my pen will never cease,
(For the more I write increase,)
If it fondly hope to tell
All the charms I love so well.
Blend the beauty thou hast known
Over mortal being thrown,
With that visioned to thy spirit,—
Faintly see then Cora's merit.

TO ———.

Great egotist and bigot! I should deem,
    Were I as void of charity as thou,
    That from a soul like thine could never flow
Such heavenly musings in melodious stream.
But I have learned that many a sunny beam,
    Just warm from heaven, steals to the earth below,
    Where opes through clouds, pitch black with hail
        and snow,
A narrow chasm with all unhoped for gleam.
And valleys where the everlasting rock
    Bounds in on every side the fettered eye,
    Reach up and up to the eternal sky;—
No limits there the eager sight doth mock.
    And the great sun o'er these contracted vales,
    As o'er the open champaign, each day sails.

THE RIVALS.

A POEM.

IN THREE PARTS.

> "Of forests and enchantments drear,
> Where more is meant than meets the ear"
>
> *Milton.*

(119)

PREFACE.

THE design of the following poem is to illustrate the conflict of a highly poetical and extremely sensitive nature with the coarser and more prosaic elements of society; and the eventual reconcilement of the poetical and prosaic, through the force of love for a common object.

The poem was written a number of years ago, and while the author is conscious that it is marred by many of the faults of youth, he cherishes the hope that it possesses some of the merits of youth also.

THE RIVALS.

PART I.

I know full well that strains of gladness
Are welcomer than those of sadness;
That joyful visions nerve the soul
When sorrows o'er it wildly roll,
To breast the torrent manfully;
That in our daily course we see
Sufficient woe, sufficient care,
Quick actions and life-long despair,
To prove, alas! that life is aught
But a gay day-dream, richly wrought
With flowers, and light, and love's embracing,
And not one shade of sorrow's tracing.

And yet it seemeth well to me
To touch at times, sweet Poësy!
Thy magic harp to mournful numbers,
And waken from their restless slumbers,
Those sad'ning strains that love to dwell
Within the bosom's inmost cell.
Oh! for me they have a pleasure
Sweeter than the lightsome measure

To whose tones the dancers move
In the gayety of love :
And the tears that fill my eye
As they tremble softly by,
And the swelling of my breast,
And my spirit's sweet unrest,
Tell that a diviner power
Floats within their hallowed hour.
And if at times that strain of sadness
    Swells to a dirge of keen despair,
And with a melancholy madness
    Flings its wild notes upon the air—
Oh! blame it not—that burst of grief
May give the anguished heart relief,
May loose the fountains of the eye
Which rolls in tearless agony,
And 'neath its soft refreshing rain,
The pallid cheek may bloom again.

What words can tell his hapless fate
    Who feels the early want of love,
Yet turns away disconsolate
    From those who round his childhood move,
With spirit crushed and faint and dim,
For no one seems to care for him !

Oh! never, from my earliest youth,
Had I a friend, a friend in truth :
Many I loved, or could have loved,
    Had they but deigned to glance on me,
And in their service would have proved
    My friendship was not vanity.
" I was a cold and quiet child"—
So thought my father, calm and mild—
He little knew— how should he know?
My childhood's agony of woe.
None but a mother's eye could trace
Beneath that still, averted face,
And in that low embarrassed tone,
And in that wish to be alone,
A heart which needed to be sought
Within its silence sorrow-fraught,
A spirit like the lava tide,
That pours down the volcano's side,
Above in cold and sluggish flow,
A fiery torrent far below.
None but a mother's heart could feel
The anguish I could ne'er reveal ;
The longing for a friendly breast,
    In which my soul like some strong river,
Might pour its flood, and be at rest,
    And flow on gently then forever.

Oh, mother ! thou wert far away,
In the glad realms of endless day ;
But didst thou not in musing hours,
Reclined on amaranthine flowers,
Feel something in thy breast which made
Even its heavenly calm afraid,
Lest one so dearly loved had need
      Of thy kind words and tender care,
To lure him from the depths which breed
      Unhappiness and wan despair ?

Thus passed my youth—the thoughtless days
When others tread a flowery maze,
      Were but a thorny path to me ;
While round me rung their laughter wild,
I was a broken-hearted child,
      The early-called of misery !
But as I grew in years and strength,
A change came over me at length ;
No longer did I mourn that none
Had been by me to friendship won ;
I gloried that my soul was proud,
And different from the vulgar crowd ;
I shunn'd the intercourse of those
Who almost seem'd my natural foes,

And in a gloomy vale apart,
Caress'd and fondled my own heart.
In nature's breast, at length I cried,
I'll find the friendship man denied ;
I'll tread with her the shadowy wood,
And lean above the foaming flood,
And hear the distant ocean roar
Against its everlasting shore,
Like the wild rushing of the blast,
(When tempests gather thick and fast,)
Through some old forest's awful shade,
Where roam the stern and mighty dead.

And nature loved me ; yes, she wore
A smile I ne'er had seen before :
I knelt beside the playful stream,
And caught full many a witching gleam
Of her dark, brilliant eye, that shone
More vivid than the diamond stone :
I sat within the dark green wood,
And gave my soul to musing mood,
And she came gently up to me
In all her wise timidity,
And whispered in my ear her love,—
I could not speak, I could not move,

11*

But in my face she read full well
The bliss my tongue could never tell.

And when the Tempest rose in might,
Like chaos from the realms of night,
And in his frenzy would have hurled
Destruction on a blooming world,
I saw with joy her lightning spear
Transfix him in his mad career,
And bear the fierce destroyer back
Upon his wild, tumultuous track,
Until he sought with many a groan,
Again his dark and heaving throne.

I stood on the volcano's side,
And felt a fierce and fearless pride,
To see the lava deluge flow
In fire upon the plains below;
Sweeping the woods away like glass,
Before its huge and glowing mass;
Filling up valleys in its path;
O'erwhelming cities in its wrath;
And rushing, with a battle cry
Like that which pealed along the sky,
When from their mountain tops at even,
The Titans stormed the gates of Heaven,

Against the dark, eternal sea,
Its everlasting enemy!

But nature cannot fill the mind ;—
It hungers after human kind.
She may beguile us for a while,
And win us with her witching smile
Where stranger's footsteps ne'er intrude,
In her sweet mountain solitude ;
But soon we feel our loneliness
Like ice upon our bosoms press.
Oh! sweetly sings the forest bird,
But sweeter far a spoken word ;
And softly azure is yon sky
        Which curtains o'er the realms of glory,
But dearer far the deep blue eye
        That pictures love's delightful story.
And then I left my forest home,
Nor longer would with nature roam :—
Think not she chided my return,
Or did me from her presence spurn.
Not so—she took me by the hand,
And led me to the open land,
Then, smiling sweetly, thus she said,
Thus softly spake the immortal maid :

" I took thee from the world apart,
That I might purify thy heart;
No mother did thy childhood know,
To share with thee the hour of woe;
I bound thee with my magic spell—
Have I not played the sister well?
Thou goest forth into the world—
Again thy spirit must be furled,
For he who flings its folds abroad,
Must wave within his hand a sword,
Upon whose bright and gleaming sail,
Vile slander's mists shall ne'er prevail,
And dash unstained and brilliantly,
From victory to victory.
But thou wast never made for this,
For the reformer's hopeful bliss;
Be thine the equal task, to win
Thy spirit from the grasp of sin;—
For he who with truth's healing tides
    Cleanses his soul from taint and scar,
Is greater than the chief who rides
    The fiery thunderbolt of war.

" I leave thee now to breast again
The world's cold blast and sleety rain;

With none to cheer thy fainting soul,
When tempests o'er it madly roll,
But that low voice which softly falls
    In dewy stillness from the sky,
Ev'n when the mighty thunder calls,
    And demon shadows cluster nigh.
Oh! would that to some child of earth,
Some maiden of a mortal birth,
My guardianship I might transfer;
How gladly would I yield to her
The pleasant task to lead thy mind
Into communion with thy kind:
I have done all a spirit could,
To make thee gentle, mild and good;
Have breathed a peace, before unknown,
O'er thy sad breast's continual moan,
And, with the beauteous hues of even,
Sought to beguile thy soul to heaven:
And now, I break the magic spell;
Be bold and true—Farewell! Farewell!"

With head advanced, and straining eye,
I listened, but could not reply;
I listened, but I could not see
The lovely nymph that spake to me:

At times a misty shadow seemed
To hover where the sunshine gleamed;
And then, beneath the forest shade,
I faintly thought a soft light played;
But when dull silence smote my ear
    With sudden and discordant tone,
I started from my trance in fear,
    And felt, alas! I was alone.
With tears I left that peaceful glen,
And sadly sought my fellow men;
Determined I would act my part
With fearless and heroic heart;
Resolved to sympathize with all;
To echo back the merry call;
To mingle with the toiling crowd,
Who madly weave their spirit's shroud;
And seek gay pleasure's world of care,
Where round white brows, so young and fair,
A wreath is flung whose fragrant breath
Is laden with remorse and death!
Yes, mingle with them all—and keep
    My spirit free from every stain—
To weep with those who sadly weep,
    And smooth the uneasy couch of pain;
And ever lend the ready hand
At truth's and charity's command;

And by my self-devotion move
Mankind to gratitude and love.

And if, oh sweet, luxurious thought!
Some gentle spirit should be brought
By love's kind angel to my side,
To be the friend my youth denied;
How gladly would I float along,
  Rocked by each moment's rosy wave,
Existence one continual song,
  Toward that port of heaven, the grave!

I sought the world; but day by day,
My hopeful visions fled away.
I could not, oh! I could not move
My fellow beings unto love!
I stood among the toiling crowd,
And called on them with accents loud,
To leave the glittering dross of earth,
And seek for things of heavenly birth:
The rich gold of a generous mind,
The pure pearls of a spirit kind,
And with all holy wishes fraught;
The flashing diamond of thought,
Which lightens through the passed-away,
Until it gleams like yesterday,

And high above, like stars, are seen
The saints and heroes that have been ;
Warriors that, giant-like, have strode
Along Fame's rough but glorious road ;
Kings, whose bright crests and waving plume,
Like foam upon a sea of gloom,
Mark where the billowy world in wrath
Has swept along its destined path ;
Seers, who above the roaring flood
Of joy and agony and blood,
Its onward course could boldly trace,
And bid the waters know their place ;
And Poets, who with gifted sight,
Proclaimed a soft, celestial light,
In the dim future breaking forth,
Like the Aurora in the north,
And touched by a prophetic power,
Sang sweetly of a coming hour,
When o'er the earth that light shall spread,
And from their tombs shall spring the dead,
And from his throne wild chaos hurled,
Shall rule no more the ransomed world.
Thus said I to the restless throng ;
And mocking laughter, loud and long,
Broke from them, as they turned again
To heap up gold and sin and pain ;

And one, with cold and glassy eye,
Cursed me aloud as I passed by.

With softened tread and stifled breath
I stood beside the couch where death
Was battling sternly for his prey;
But youth will wrestle manfully ;
For hope is strong, and love still clings
    To the low grove where first it sung,
Nor pants to soar on golden wings,
    The rosy clouds of heaven among.
It is an awful thing to stand
    By the dim couch in such an hour,
And feel the dying's icy hand
    Grasp yours with a convulsive power ;
And mark the changes that denote
    That life's sad flame is burning dim,
The low quick gasping of the throat,
    The quivering of the lip and limb.
Oh ! thoughts will press upon you then
Of many an unrepented sin ;
Of words you have in anger spoken
    To him who now before you lies,
The last slight fetter nearly broken,
    That holds his spirit from the skies !
12

But he, by whose low bed I stood,
Ne'er suffered from my angry mood ;
No friend nor relative of mine
　　　Was he upon whose pallid cheek
Was written many a fearful sign
　　　That death was strong and life was weak.
For weeks, beside that sick man's bed,
With anxious eye and careful tread,
And strength no watching could abate,
I hung upon his doubtful fate.
'Twas mine to bathe his burning face,
To give him drink, to shift his place,
And gratify his every whim ;
What man could do I did for him.
At length a cool, refreshing sleep
　　　Rested upon the sick man's brow,
So calm, so peaceful and so deep,
　　　We knew that life had triumphed now ;
And from that hour he mended fast,
Each day was stronger than the last,
And soon he left his humble door
With step as vigorous as before.

I sought that man in after days,
When, through blind fortune's devious ways,

Of him and his I stood in need;
But " he was busy then, indeed!"
There was *this* thing that must be done,
And *that*, before to-morrow's sun;
His children, too, they must be fed,—
" No! let them starve!" I sternly said;
And turned away, in bitter scorn
That such a wretch was ever born.

Oh! who, in court, or lady's bower,
Can tell the secret of that power,
By which the happiness of one
  Is bound unto another's heart,
So that a word, a glance, a tone
  Can joy or misery impart!
Oh, who can read that witching spell,
  Which beauty o'er her worshippers,
Flings from the soft eye's dreamy cell,
  Until your very soul is hers,
And in her service you would press
  Where life is crowded with the brave,
And dare all but forgetfulness,
  That doom more dreadful than the grave.

Yes! even now, that form of light
Floats like a dream before my sight:

Again I see that face where love
Sat softly brooding like a dove;
The cheek's luxurious repose,
Whose virgin freshness shamed the rose;
And the rich curls whose sunny fall
Flung a soft radiance over all!
But not in these, though these alone
Around my heart a spell had thrown,
So full of passion and of might,
I lived but in its wild delight;
But in her calm and tranquil mood,
So free from guile, so meek, so good;—
The innocency of her breast,
Where gentle longings lay at rest,
Like snow-white lambs, at noontide seen
Upon some cool and shady green;
The trusting hopefulness of youth,
So full of purity and truth,
Which listens with a doubting sense,
Born of its love-full confidence,
Unto the warning voice of age,
Telling of man's deceit and rage;—
Oh! in these spiritual charms
    I saw that holy radiance shine,
To which my childhood stretched its arms,
    With feelings it could not define!

Day after day I sought her side,
And every soft allurement tried
To win her love, that I might be
No more the child of misery.
At length I thought her tender heart
Was yielding to the lover's art;
Her tone grew softer when I came,
Her cheek would color at my name,
And from my own her clear blue eye
Would turn with love's timidity;
At least I thought so, though perchance
It was but my enraptured glance,
Which with its passionate reply,
Caused her to turn, she knew not why.
And yet at times, when she would start
At the wild words which from my heart
Came rushing, free and strong and bold,
Like waves that would not be controlled,
And look upon me as with fear,
I thought I was no longer dear;
And cursed the mood that might have driven
My soul from her and love and heaven.

Some months, perhaps a year, passed by;
   It seem'd nor long nor short to me;
12*

For when the pulse is beating high,
And o'er the heart swift feelings fly,
In the mad revelry of strife,
When passion strains the chords of life,
Or in that wild and thrilling hour
When first we pluck love's virgin flower,—
    Time is not, but Eternity !

That year—or was it but a day ?
To live was more than to decay !
Its memory comes o'er me now
Like a cool breeze upon my brow ;
And though my life has been a scene,
    From youth to age, of more than pain,
For that bewildering hour between,
    I'd live it o'er again !

For I was ever by her side ;
Exulting with a lover's pride,
As some new charm, from hour to hour,
Sprang forth and blossomed like a flower.
We trod together the green wood,
And by the sparkling fountain stood,
And hand in hand we climbed the hill,
Or followed gayly the sweet rill,

That like a merry-hearted child,
Wanders alone through thickets wild,
Through valleys, and through meadows green,
Hiding as fearful to be seen,
And laughs along its truant way
At those who would have said it nay!
And yet, though we were thus alone
Where nature's softly varied tone,
The flowery earth, the sky above,
Dispose the youthful heart to love,
Ah, never did I dare to speak
Of love unto that maiden meek.
Although no longer did she shrink
    From the wild frenzy of my fever,
Like the lone wanderer from the brink
    Of some unseen, dark whirling river;
But would with many a soothing word,
Sweet as the carol of a bird,
Restrain my passion's fierce excess,
And conquer pride with tenderness,
Yet could I not persuade my heart
She acted more than a sister's part;
And thus I feared to speak to her
Like what I was, her worshipper,
Lest in my boldness I should sever
The bond between our souls forever:

And if some holy power of heaven,
Had to my heart assurance given,
That I might always live as then
In that unknown, sequestered glen,
And thus through life's dark waters glide
Forever by her lovely side,
I would have crushed without a sigh,
My longings for a nearer tie,
And thanked the God of Light above,
For my sweet sister's gentle love !

THE RIVALS.

PART II

Deep in the soul the tree of life is planted,
    From whose fair branches heavenly virtues spring;
But round the cavern'd boughs, by angels haunted,
    Poisonous vines, like hideous serpents, cling;
One moment—opens a sweet bud of glory;
    The next—there blooms a cold and deadly flower;
And the soft murmur of love's blissful story,
    Blends with the frenzy of the battle hour.
The winds may strive to banish hate and sorrow,
    The waters seek to cleanse the tainted soul,
And solitude earth's holiest music borrow,
    But the fierce serpent mocks their vain control.

—

Among my schoolmates, there was one
Whose presence I did ever shun;
I know not why it was, but he
Was always hateful unto me:
His every tone of joy or fear,
Grated on my averted ear;

(141)

His look of triumph and of pride,
Wakened disgust I could not hide ;
And as I yielded to its power,
It on me grew from hour to hour,
Until I loathed, yes, even more
Than aught that I had known before,
More than the slimy worm which crawls
On some old temple's ruined walls,—
Oh God of mercy, spare thy ban !
This child of thine, my brother man !

You ask if in his bosom dwelt
The same aversion which I felt ;
No ! for his breast was calm and cold,
Compared to mine ; his feelings rolled
Like a dull river o'er a plain,
Inert and sluggish to the main :
His soul was never made to thrill
With the extremes of good and ill,
To mount upon hope's blessed wing,
Where seraph and archangel sing,
Or, in fear's horrid arms, to leap
Where things obscene and loathsome creep,
And hear, like a dull, distant knell,
The dreadful revelry of hell.

That want of sympathy, which broke
Upon me like a thunder-stroke,
So that I felt his very tread,
And from his coming footsteps fled,
Upon him came with feebler burst:
He felt no loathing at the first;
None of that deep, instinctive hate,
Which all my will could not abate;
But by degrees within his mind
A cold dislike, uncaused and blind,
Which misinterpreted my deeds,
And found no flower among the weeds,
Grew up, and he accosted me,
With slight, repelling courtesy.

In all the hopes that boyhood hath,
That boy was ever in my path:
He was the only one who could
Rival my aim in the wild wood;
He was as fleet of foot as I,
Could fling the ball as far and high,
And in our school-hours none could see
That either had the mastery.
But he was loved, alas! by all,
And I was loved by none—their call

Would ring out gayly, when the gush
Of merry voices broke the hush
Of the still school, for him, their head,
Prepared to follow where he led :
While I would sadly steal away
Unnoticed from the eager play,
And seek some lone, secluded spot,
To weep o'er my unhappy lot :
And ofttimes through my brain would steal
The thought, too bitter far to heal,
That if he only would depart,
I then might gain the general heart,
(For of the rest no one could hope
With me in skill or strength to cope,)
And by my fearless daring move
My reckless comrades unto love.

And when from nature's holy fane
I slowly turned, to tread again
'Mid scenes of cold and heartless joy,
I met him, now no more a boy.
But time, though it had left its trace
In the fixed muscles of the face,
And changed the stripling's slender form
        To manhood's broad and noble bearing,

Prepared to breast the wrathful storm,
　　And never fail for want of daring,
Had not removed his cold dislike,
Which would condemn, but would not strike,
Nor my aversion, scarcely hid,
To all he said, or looked, or did.

It was a lovely summer night:
The moon looked down in calm delight
　　Upon a hushed and tranquil world;
The earth lay sleeping like a child,
Over whose features undefiled,
Glides with a pure, seraphic gleam,
The light trace of a heavenly dream;
　　And ev'n the storm cloud which lay furled
In the low bosom of the west,
Seemed charmed to peacefulness and rest
By the soft silvery smile which played
Within its black and rugged shade,
Like a young maiden, bright and good,
Within some old and dark-browed wood.
I had been kept by men away
From Helen's presence all the day;
Had mingled in their empty strife,
And fought as if for fame and life;

13

And as I hastened to her side,
I dwelt with rapture and with pride
On the kind welcome which would greet
The sound of my approaching feet.
I gazed upon the scene around,
Where each discordant shape was drowned
In a clear flood of dewy light;
And thought, thus has my heart of night
Been overflowed by radiant love,
From the pure fount of bliss above.
But ere that thought's ethereal trace
      Had vanished from my mind like breath,
A change came over nature's face,
      A change like that from life to death.
One moment—to the fresh'ning gale
The hillside spreads its gleaming sail;
Another comes—and where is now
The dazzling mount's majestic brow,
The valley, and the silvery flow
Of waters, murmuring soft and low ?
All! all are fled! and where they stood,
Rolled a black ocean's sullen flood;
And like a wreck above it shone
With ghastly light the cold grave-stone :
Yes! glaring through the ebon gloom,
The only beacon was the tomb!

Why was it that I turned my head,
And looked behind me as in dread?
Why from my breast did gladness flee?
Was it that dark cloud's witchery?
Why should I mind a passing cloud?
It wraps the earth though like a shroud;
And the fierce storm-winds, as they fly,
With shrill, wild laughter, echo, why?

I stood beside the well-known door:
    Why did I stand irresolute?
I ne'er had felt as then before :—
    Was that the low tone of a flute?
It was! and hark, it breathes again,
And pours its rich, melodious strain.
Oh! never did a funeral bell
Toll such a sad, desponding knell,
As that proud strain, so bold and clear,
Sounded upon my fearful ear! .
At length, with slow and noiseless tread,
And hardly knowing what I did,
I gained a window where the light
Streamed out upon the solid night,
And hid within the curtaining gloom,
Gazed fearfully into the room.

There sat, and as I gazed my blood
Swept through me like an icy flood,
And for a moment's space my brain
Swam dizzily with intensest pain,
Yes! seated by my Helen's side,
And gazing on her in his pride,
In pride that has in love its birth,
The man I hated most on earth!

Ye who have seen a comrade fall
Beneath your own accursed ball;
Ye who have stood beside the bier,
And shed the unavailing tear
Over the sire your deeds of gloom
Have brought in sorrow to the tomb;
Or who have knelt beside the grave
Of her you would have died to save;
And felt that sinking of the heart,
That wish that life would then depart,
That you might sleep, and feel no more
The woe you only could deplore;
May understand the deep despair,
The agony which smote me there!

With faltering step I turned away:
I could not weep, I could not pray,

I could not reason what was best,
When on my brain such madness press'd :
I turned me from that once-loved door,
Which I might never enter more ;—
What did I care that round my path
The lightning quivered in its wrath !
With scornful smile I stretched my hand
To grasp it, as it were a wand ;
What cared I that the thunder sped
In sharp, quick volleys o'er my head ?
I stood erect, nor bowed my form
Before the demon of the storm,
And dreaded not his vengeful spear ;—
For grief, like love, can cast out fear !

Ere long upon my fevered brain,
The knowledge fell like fiery rain,
That my forebodings were not vain :
That eve was not the first that he,
Now doubly known my enemy,
Had met with her whose every tone
I had so longed to call my own.
He was the chosen of her bower
In girlhood's young and timid hour ;
And when that budding spring-time fled,
And the new glory round her head,

13*

And the soft eye's redoubled power,
Told womanhood began to flower,
She gave to him her gentle heart,
Without restraint or fear or art ;
And when at duty's stern command,
He lingering left his native land,
She dried her tears and banished pain,
And gave to hope the silken rein,
And waited with a holy trust
In the eternal and the just,
For the sweet hour when he should come
On love's swift pinions to her home,
And in her warm embrace forget
The tedious months since last they met.

And I had met her in those hours,
When o'er her bosom's early flowers
A cloud had passed, beneath whose shade
She dwelt in peace, and not afraid,
But with a gentler (could it be ?)
Sense of her own sweet dignity ;—
And while I gazed upon her face,
Enraptured with each lovely grace,
Her absent thoughts were far away ;
His form was near her, day by day ;

His voice forever in her ear,
　With its cold tones, to her so dear,
And his that musing mood which proves
That she who feels it truly loves.
I never sought her presence more ;
　I could not meet her as before ;
And he was ever by her side,
And soon would claim her as his bride.
How could she bear to look on one,
　And own him as her being's sun,
From whom my every sense shrunk back,
As from a serpent's hated track ?
How could she press the very hand,
　That I recoiled from as a brand
Flashing before the startled sight,
Within some forest's gloomy light ?
How could she love the loud cold tone,
　So harsh, and different from her own,
So calm, self-confident and bold,
That of a coarse nature told,
And jarred upon my every sense,
And filled me. with disgust intense.

But she did love him, and for me
　　There was no further happiness :

I was "upon a wide, wide sea,
  Alone ! alone !" with none to bless :
And yet, upon my heart at first,
That dreadful knowledge did not burst
With the same fearful, blasting power
That smote it in a later hour.
No ! as upon the west at even
Linger the rosy tints of Heaven,
Ev'n when the sun has fled the sight,
And with its chill embrace the night
Has in her gloom and stillness come
To make the awe-struck world her home ;
So on my darkening soul I ween,
Lingered the glory that had been,
And with its softly fading ray,
Smoothed the departure of the day.

But soon upon my bosom came,
Like an uncurbed, destroying flame,
The mournful memory of the past ;—
The bliss that I had won at last ;
The few short hours of love and gladness,
When from my spirit fled its sadness ;
And that dread moment of despair,
When, with a fixed, unearthly stare,

And breathings that came thick and slow,
While cold drops gathered on my brow,
I gazed with sad and hopeless glance,
  Upon that sight which told me all,
Like one who, wakening from his trance,
  Sees the tomb's cold and slimy wall.

I sought again, I know not why,
  The paths that I with her had trod :
There was the same still, azure sky,
  There was the freshly springing sod ;
The streamlet seemed to bound along
As full of life, as full of song ;
The breezes played around my head
A moment and then onward fled ;
I heard, as they came fast and nigh,
Their waving garments rustle by :
Yes, nature, careless nature, wore
The same glad aspect as before.
But I was changed, and could not see
The beauty which had raptured me,
When with an angel for my guide,
I had explored the mountain side ;
The sky then o'er me seemed to bend
Kind as an old, familiar friend,

The brook its sweetest music brought
To wreathe around each lovely thought,
The breeze would come with fingers fair
And kindly part my floating hair,
And all around me seemed to tell
With varied grace they loved me well.
But now no welcome met my ear,
No joyful song, no whisper dear;
The playful breeze, and ev'n the brook,
Passed by me with averted look;
They cared no more—why should they care?
For him who wandered sadly there.
The sunshine on my dazzled sight
Glared with a cold, unearthly light;
I turned, and sought the forest shade,
But its deep gloom and stillness weighed
Upon my spirit in that hour,
With undefined though dreadful power;
Until I left with aching breast,
The paths I once so gladly pressed,
And felt their beauty had departed
With her, the pure and gentle hearted!
At length, with a determined mind
I said, this grief no more shall bind
My spirit in its mournful cell;
In foreign lands I'll break the spell,

Forget what has been, as a dream
That eddies on sleep's glassy stream,
And o'er the earth a wanderer roam,
Nor ask its millions for a home.
But though I often said : " to-morrow,
And I will leave this land of sorrow,"
I never could resolve to go,
Until I heard that word of woe,
That she I loved had pledged her faith,
That faith which woman keeps till death,
To him who from my childhood's hour,
    So oft had clouded o'er my day,
And trampled on the only flower
    That ever bloomed along my way.

I know 'twas very weak, but I
Before that hour could never fly.
I had no hope that she could be
What she had been again to me ;
And yet as clings the swimmer's hand,
Even in dying, to the sand
On which he lies, far, far below
The upper wave's tumultuous flow ;
As turns the exile to the shore
Whose borders he shall see no more,

And dreams that in the distant sky,
And its light, cloudy drapery,
He still beholds his native land;
So turned my eye, and clung my hand,
To that last hope, which hope was none,
That sunshine from a perished sun.

No longer did I wish delay:
The only tie was rent away
That bound me to my native earth:
For me there blazed no household hearth;
No sister's lip was pressed to mine;
No mother for her son would pine;
And what cared I if o'er my head
My country's brilliant azure spread;
Or darker skies, whose dismal light
Scarce differed from another night?
Oh blame me not, my native clime!
That I forgot thee for a time;
For soon upon my breast returned
The love I had so madly spurned:
For who can long forget the sod
On which his boyish footsteps trod;
The shadowy wood, so dark and still;
The wide-spread meadow, and the rill

Round which in childish glee he played,
And sported with the slight cascade;
The tree upon whose giant breast
He nestled from the lowering west,
And smiled to see the lightning fly
On strong and flashing pinions by;
The lake within whose cooling wave
His heated form at eve he'd lave,
While with the excess of joy he laughed,
As every pore the nectar quaffed;
The hills within whose caverned sides
Even at noon no sunbeam glides,
And where with slow and solemn tread
He ventured, filled with awe and dread;
Yet felt withal a fearful pleasure,
Like one who seeks a buried treasure,
By the cold stars uncertain light,
While clouds sweep o'er the gusty night;—
Oh who these memories can efface
     With ruthless violence from his brain,
And leave within no lovely trace
     Of that which ne'er may be again!

I stood upon the vessel's side,
And waited for the sluggish tide,
     14

To bear me from my native clime,
And her whom now to love were crime.
I felt no more the keen distress,
The fiery flood of bitterness
Which flowed upon me when I woke
In anguish from the thunder stroke,
Only to wish that I had died
By that which smote me from her side.
Now, when I thought of her, my heart
Oft linked by a mysterious art,
Her image with his odious form ;
A rosebud and a loathsome worm
They seemed to my distempered thought;
And though her memory was fraught
At times with the sweet calm of heaven,
It seemed, oh may I be forgiven!
In other stormier moods, so clothed
With his whose very name I loathed,
That I with scorn would oft repel
The thought of her once loved so well.

At length our broad and fluttering sail
Caught to its heaving breast the gale,
And panting with its keen delight,
Sprang forth on its uncertain flight ;

And as my native mountains fell
Behind the ocean's distant swell,
I thought of those I left behind,
The noble hearted! and the kind!
At least they seemed so then, for ne'er
Had they before been thought so dear,—
Nor knew I, till I left its strand,
How much I loved my native land.

But while my eyes were filled with tears,
And swayed my heart with hopes and fears,
I slowly turned—can that be he
Whose presence I had hoped to flee?
Must he forever follow me?
No! I was not deceived; that tread
Above my dull and buried head,
Would wake me from my dreamless sleep,
And through my veins the blood would creep
In cold slow drops, and yet too fast,
Until his careless step had passed:
No, I was not deceived, that form,
Though now with youth and triumph warm,
I should mistake not, though it press'd
That shadowy undefined of rest,
Which the dim phantoms of the dead
With half-unconscious footsteps tread,

Until at the great Trumpet's call,
They darken round the judgment hall.

I heard, though not till after time,
IIis parents lived in the olden clime;
And at their summons he had said
Farewell to her whom he had wed
But one short, blissful month before,
That they might see his face once more.

But as it chanced, I knew not then
Why he had left that lovely glen,
And her whose heavenly presence made
The sunshine as a pleasant shade;
The shadow as a glorious light;
The noonday as the spangled night;
The midnight as a glowing morn,
A dewy rosebud, newly born,
And flinging fragrance all around,
Upon the air, upon the ground,
Until we faint with its excess
Of odorous deliciousness.

Oh 'tis a glorious thing to sail
   Upon the vast and mighty sea;
   14*

And bid its snow-capped billows hail,
    The emblems of the truly free!
Unlike the Andes' rocky form,
Scarce yielding to the moulding storm,
And which in stubborn strength defies
The influence of centuries;
Unlike the worthless creeds of old,
Rooted in custom's clinging mould,
And which in dreadful fetters bind
Alike the body and the mind;
They sway with every impulse given
By the soft wind, the breath of heaven,
And follow on the earth their wise
And meek-eyed leader of the skies!

Day after day we sailed along
Before that breeze so fresh and strong,
Until the seventh morning broke
Upon the sea in vapory smoke.
Hoarse moaned the billows: and the sun
Rose from the gory wave as one
Who all the night with furious tread,
Among the dying and the dead,
Had swept along the battle plain,
And marked his pathway by the slain.
    14*

Yes, like a warrior king he rose,
Who hears the hated tread of foes,
And calls his subjects from afar,
To join the dreadful ranks of war;
And at his bidding, overhead
His dark terrific legions spread,
With swift yet silent march they poured
Around the banner of their lord,
Then flung its sable folds abroad,
And waved on high the lightning sword,
And down the black vault of the sky
Rushed with their fierce artillery.
The earth stood still, when on it first
The rattling thunder madly burst,
As if the massive arch of Heaven
From its foundations had been riven,
And with a crashing, heavy sound,
Had fallen to the vast profound.
The earth stood still, like one who hears
A strange, dread sound with sudden fears,
And then with an unearthly cry,
Bounds on his path in agony :—
So sprung all nature from its trance,
And casting round a fearful glance,
Rushed madly on, it knew not where,
Wild with its terror and despair.

Our vessel reeled beneath the blast,
Which drove her without sail or mast,
Like a thin cloud where'er it would;
For we had done what mortals could,
And waited now in dread suspense,
The stern decree of Providence.

It was a strange and dreadful sight
That met us, when the livid light
Flashed forth at times that awful night:
Oh! there were men bowed down in prayer
That God their guilty lives would spare,
Who never had bent the stubborn knee
Since the frolic hours of infancy,
When, at the holy even tide,
They knelt by their dear mother's side,
With guileless heart and sinless brow,
And prayed for that they needed now.
And there was a boy with a manly heart,
Who did not fear from life to part,
But by his pale young sister stood,
So meek and beautiful and good!
And whispered words of hope and cheer;
But she could not restrain the struggling tear;
Not that she dreaded to die, oh no!
When her Father called she was ready to go;

But there was one in a distant land,
To whom she had plighted her heart and hand,
And she thought how sadly, day by day,
He would look for her who was far away,
And the frenzy of his heart and brain,
When he should hear that ne'er again
He might behold the eye that shone
Always on him, on him alone.
And there was a mother, who sternly press'd
Her sleeping infant to her breast,
(For midst fearful sight and anguished tone,
That innocent child still slumbered on,)
And with her shawl she had bound it there,
That not even the waves from her side should tear
The gentle flower that had been given
Unto her prayers by love and Heaven.
And there were two who stood apart,
Cheek pressed to cheek, and heart to heart;
Their bosoms felt no wild alarms,
For they were in each other's arms;
They did not fear the stormy weather,
If they might only die together;
And she had torn her belt in haste
From round her softly moulded waist,
And bade him bind them so that they
Might like one spirit pass away.

The morning dawned, and with it came
A whispered fear, that spread like flame;
They said the ship was sinking fast;
" Another hour must be the last!"
Then strong men pushed the weak aside,
With dreadful oaths, to which replied
Low smothered curses, (such as chill
The heart when all is bright and still,
But with that awful sky o'erhung,
Curdled my blood,) and madly sprung
Into the boat, which the wild sea
   Tossed in its fierce, capricious play,
   Like a panther sporting with his prey,
Till it was crowded fearfully.

With threats and menaces at last
They loosed the rope that held us fast,
And rowed where we might safely mark
The fierce death struggle of our bark.
Oh never may man hear again
Such supplications made in vain,
As we were forced to hear from those
O'er whom the waves were soon to close :
They begged that we would save them, we
Who every moment feared the sea

Our heavy laden boat would fill :
They heeded not our words, but still
Implored and prayed that we would save
Them from the stern, remorseless wave :
But others stood in calm despair,
With those they loved all gathered there,
Sustained by an eternal power
Through that slow-paced and dreadful hour.

At length a loud and fearful sound,
Like the last death shriek of the drowned
Before he sinks beneath the wave,
Burst from the ship, as from a grave ;
And then more dreadful than that cry,
Was the shrill scream of agony,
Which from those hapless wretches came,
And wild appealings to His name,
Whose voice could calm the raging sea
Of dark, tempestuous Galilee ;
And then an awful stillness spread
Over the scene, as with a dread,
Convulsive start that vessel sprung,
With all the souls that to her clung,
Beneath the waves, and left no trace
To mark her fearful resting place,

Save the strong whirlpool's sudden swell,
Save the dark water's mournful knell,
Save the sad memories that roam
From the now lone and quiet home,
And weave their melancholy song,
All tearful as they float along,
Above the ocean tomb where lie
The loved and young of days gone by!

One crowded boat alone was left:
A hundred beings had been reft
Of life and motion, and the sea
Had closed above them eagerly;
One shattered boat, without a sail,
Which reeled beneath the abating gale,
Alone remained of all the pride
Which winds and waves alike defied,
And seemed a thing of beauty, sent
A queen for that wild element!

Was it not strange that he and I
    Were both among that small boat-crew?
It seemed to me he could not die
    Save by the bolt that smote me too.
Yet even in that dreadful hour
Our hate had scarcely lost its power;

Far apart as stern from prow,
He and I were seated now ;
And not a word of hope or fear,
Not even a glance, to soothe or cheer,
Parted his lips, or lit my eye,
During that hour of agony.

Our boat unmanageable lay
Upon the waters till noonday ;
Then a rough sailor and untaught,
Spake out aloud what all had thought :
He said that some must die, or none
Could hope to reach the shore ; the sun
Now shone with cold and gloomy light,
But all foretold a stormy night :
" Let us cast lots"—with trembling hold
Each took the fluttering slip, that told
Whether his course was yet to be
A little longer on the sea,
Or whether to his briny foe
He should some minutes sooner go :—
They rise, that brave, devoted band !
And for a moment silent stand,
Gazing upon the sky, the main,
And all they ne'er shall see again

An instant, for a hurried prayer,
Another, and but one is there;
A slender boy, who clasps his hands,
And in a death-like stupor stands,
(It is so hard for youth to die,
And leave the world's sweet melody!)
Then plunges 'neath the opening tide,
The purest yet the last who died.

Was it not strange that I and he,
Who was ev'n yet my enemy,
Were still among the favored few
To whom capricious fate was true?
For now with long and lusty pull,
We skimmed the waves like the sea-gull,
And ere an hour, oh joyful sight!
The clouds rolled from the heavens so bright;
And from their sable folds their lord
Sprung flashing like an unsheathed sword;
Burning above with diamond blaze,
Which dazzled our enfeebled gaze;
And far away within the west,
Above the dark wave's sparkling crest,
We saw a speck of deeper blue
Than ever winds or waters knew;

15

And then a shout of triumph sprung,
Like Hope unfettered, from the young ;
And the old smiled, and from their eyes
Wiped tears of gladness and surprise.
But even in that joyful glow
I turned not kindly to my foe ;
Once, when I looked with kindling glance
Upon each happy countenance,
My eye met his ; I coldly frowned,
And turned with haughty heart around ;
And as I turned, a shadow cold
Flung o'er the earth its gloomy fold :
I thought a moment that the sky
Frowned on my bitter enmity.

We neared the land—it was an isle
Where rocks in wild confusion pile
Their threat'ning forms, like dragons dread,
With flaming scales and eyes of red,
Which guard from sinful step and hand,
The gorgeous realms of fairy land :
And dismal caverns, opening wide
Their horrid jaws, we faintly spied,
Where with a low, convulsive roar
Against the stern and rugged shore,

The shuddering waves were fiercely hurled
By the mad demon of the world.
And now our boat was forced along
As by some spirit, fierce and strong,
Towards that high and rocky coast ;
And the billows howled, lost! lost!
And madly leaped around our way,
Exulting in their vengeful play.
But hark—what means that sudden cry
From thy compressed depths, agony!
A rood before the boat there lay,
Like a fiend watching for his prey,
A sharp black rock, so covered o'er
That none had noticed it before ;—
And now it was too late, one sweep
  Of the stern waves, and we were flung,
  The weak and strong, the old and young,
Into the madly whirling deep.
As tired men to a heavy sleep,
So yielded most unto the main,
Outworn with toil, unnerved by pain ;
But others would not yield their breath
So tamely to the vampire death ;
With frenzied arms they struck the wave,
And called on those who could not save,

Struggling to reach the boat, which still
Lay on the waters, tossed at will,
As some have struggled for a crown,
Until she filled and soon went down;
And then they knew that hope was none,
And sank despairing, one by one,
Till only two were left with me
To breast that rough, tremendous sea.

Was it not strange that he and I
Were thrown together thus to die?
To die! and yet our strength may serve
        To reach perchance that distant shore;
We can but fail, strain every nerve,
        For ne'er had you such cause before.
With lusty arms we threw aside
The opposing waves, and like a tide
Bore us right nobly tow'rd the land;
        But ere our journey's half was done,
Our comrade's weak and failing hand
        Told that his course was almost run:
We could not help him, and he knew
It were but our destruction too;
He asked it not, but slowly sank
Beneath the infuriate waves, which drank

His struggling being up with fiendish laughter,
Then turned with furious howls, and hurried after
Those who still fled upon the treacherous flood,
Fierce as a tiger that has tasted blood.

With arms that weak and weaker grew
    With every stroke, we neared the shore;
And not too soon, for well I knew
    That I had sunk outworn before,
    Had it not been for a broken oar
That some relenting wave had flung
Within my reach; and then I sprung
With slackening sinews newly strung,
Towards that rocky coast and bare;
But hold—where is my comrade—where?
I turned, and saw him faintly meeting
The waves which over him were beating,
Perishing there within a rood
Where he in safety might have stood:
With hasty strokes I gained his side,
And with a sudden gush of pride,
Gave to his grasp my buoyant oar;
Then turned again and sought the shore,
Aiding with weak but ready hand,
My enemy unto the land.
    15*

A wild and swollen wave at length
Flung us with its resistless strength
Upon the shore, and there we lay,
With hardly strength to crawl away
From its returning flood ;
We crept from danger as we could,
Then yielded to the mist which spread
Before our eyes, the rock our bed,
And slept as only they may sleep,
Who have been battling with the deep.

When I awoke, the morning sun
His daily course had just begun ;
And my companion slumbered still ;
But yet not soundly, for a thrill
Of pleasure oft would come and go
On his thin cheek and pallid brow.
Perchance he dreams of one whose name
Quivers within my heart like flame ;
Perchance he now in fancy presses
Her to his breast, with fond caresses,
And hears like music from above,
The softly thrilling tones of love.
It maddened me to think that she
Should be beloved by such as he ;

Had I been he, I would have died,
(I muttered in my scornful pride,)
Before I would existence owe
To one whom I had thwarted so.
He still slept on, and fearing lest
My angry words should break his rest,
I left him slumbering on the shore,
And turned me inland to explore
What glorious shapes or beings vile,
Dwelt on that rock-engirdled isle.

Hour after hour I toiled in vain
To gain the summit of the chain
Of lofty rocks, which boldly stand
Around that wave-encircled land,
Like knights of old with weapons bare,
Around the Fairest of the Fair,
A dauntless few, among a rude
And weak and cowardly multitude,
Bearing them back with lance in rest,
Stern, silent, cool and self-possessed.
At length I reached the highest peak;
And lo! the scene—but words are weak
To picture such a vision bright
As spread before my raptured sight;

Valleys, and hills, and mighty trees
Which there had grown for centuries;
And tiny streams, which flowed in mirth,
The sunbeams of a radiant earth!
And sparkling lakes, which shone like stars;
And sunshine, which in golden cars
Fled lightly 'fore the chasing wind,
Like hope's bright visions through the mind:
But not a human form appeared;
No mighty fane, nor palace, reared
Its haughty head against the sky;
No humble cottage timidly
Raised its meek forehead from the earth,
        As if it had no right to be,
And those who crowded round its hearth
        Were born for chains and misery;
It seemed as if no foot of man
Had ever stamped the primal ban
Upon the fair, angelic brow
        Of that meek, Eden-featured isle;
As if no earthly eye till now,
        Its perfect beauty might defile:
And as I left my mountain height,
And wandered, filled with calm delight,
Within the valley's beauteous shade,
A moment on my spirit weighed

The sad'ning thought, that with me came
A spark of that destroying flame,
Which o'er the earth so oft has spread
With rapid and vindictive tread,
Blasting the beauty God has given
To make this world a second heaven.

I found at length a fitting spot,
And built myself a little cot
To shield me from the midnight dew,
    And thus I passed my days :
In the fresh morning, I would woo
      The rising sun's health-giving rays,
And scan the ocean's circling blue,
Hoping the gleam would meet my view
      Of an approaching sail;
Then as the sun went up the sky,
Into the forest would I fly,
      And bid its cool recesses hail!
When evening came with timid tread,
Covered o'er with rosy red,
Like a newly-wedded bride
Blushing to her lover's side,
With a starry diamond sparkling
      On her gently-swelling breast,

Growing bolder with the dark'ning,
　　Now caressing and carest,
Then I sought the open valley,
　　And the loud resounding shore,
Heard the billows' distant rally,
　　And their dull and heavy roar.

Another cottage also stood
　　Now on that fair enchanted isle;
Mine in the shadow of a wood
　　Was reared; his in the brazen smile
Of the bold sun, upon a green
Level and smooth as e'er was seen,
Where not a tree with breezy play
Fanned the heated brow of day;
And there he had enclosed a space
From the sweet quiet of the place,
For living being there was none
Whose presence he had need to shun,
And gathered in its narrow bound
All that with keenest search he found,
By careful nature kindly lent
For raiment or for nourishment.
He wandered oft that island round,
With sharp eyes fixed upon the ground,

Exploring each sequestered haunt,
For herb of power and useful plant,
And bearing them with pride away,
Elated with his petty prey.
I smiled in scorn to see him tread
Where all around and overhead,
Nature had graven words of might,
Of holy promise and delight,
Unconscious of the shapes which press
With airy tread the wilderness,
But cannot their sweet message tell
  Until the mortal of their love,
Breaks with his quick desire the spell,
  And with them mounts to realms above.
Hark! even now I hear their song,
Shrinking, as it floats along,
From the rugged voice of day :
" Weary mortal! come away!
Leave the body and its cares,
Leave its sorrows and despairs ;
We do neither toil nor spin,
Yet are, mortal! free from sin ;
We are useless in the sight,
Idling thus from morn till night,
Of the man who cannot see
Visions of eternity

Flashing through this earthly shroud,
Like the lightning through a cloud ;
But are messengers of bliss
Unto him who feels that this
Outward world, in vapory lightness,
Rolls before the eternal brightness,
Veiling from his feeble eyes
The dazzling glory of the skies!"

Thus months flew by ; and not a word
Of joy or sorrow ever stirred
The still air of that lonely isle ;
We met, and passed, without a smile,
Without a glance to tell that we
Were children of one family :
The wild bird, floating in the air,
Turned if it met another there,
And flew in joyful circles round
The glossy treasure it had found ;
And timorous creatures of the wood,
A moment's space uncertain stood,
Then to each other's side drew nigh
With mute, unconscious sympathy ;
But we with scornful glance drew back
From one another's hated track,

And turned with hasty steps aside,
Whene'er we heard the well-known stride.

I said that we had never spoken :
    I had forgotten—once we met
When words of sorrow would have broken
    From lips where nature's seal was set.
It was upon a rocky height,
Where every morning with the light
I came, to sweep with eager glance
The ocean's spherical expanse,
Hoping some sail would meet my view
Amid the vast and tiresome blue,
Like a white, sunlit wing at even,
Flashing in depths of the eastern heaven!
That morn my foe had also sought
The ocean with accordant thought;
And, as he passed me carelessly,
Still gazing on the distant sea,
He gave a sudden start, and cried
" A sail! a sail!" forgot was pride—
Forgot was every feeling then
But longing for our fellow men :
We waved our garments in the air ;
At first, with hope ; then, with despair ;
16

For still the vessel kept her way
Right onward through the glistening spray,
Bounding along the heaving sea,
With light and graceful witchery :
And then we shouted, long and loud ;
But still she passed on, like a cloud,
A fairy cloud ! that speeds along
Unto the west wind's happy song,
Unmindful that sad hearts are aching,
Weak spirits faltering, strong ones breaking,
So filled with its own blessed lot,
That others' sorrows are forgot.

A year passed by ; I had become
Contented with my island home ;
'Tis true I longed at times to stand
Again upon my native land,
And every morning as before,
I early sought the ocean shore.
And woe to him who from his heart
Can madly pluck that better part,
And fling it carelessly aside :
For soon that cottage, once his pride,
Will lose the charm that made it dear ;
No more, upon his tuneless ear,

Will fall the soothing strains of love;
And o'er the wide world, like the Dove
O'er the earth-covering waters, he shall fly,
And find no rest from its immensity!
But time, though it had worn the chain
Which bound me to my native plain,
Had not made love or friendship grow
Between me and my hated foe.
We met within the wood no more,
Nor on the ocean's rocky shore:
One half, he knew, of the sweet isle,
Was his, to sully and defile;
There, he might slyly creep along,
And strike the minstrel, while his song
Was gushing from his ardent throat,
In many a long and liquid note,
Winding around the breathless air,
In soft melodious folds, its fetters fair.
There, trembling things might steal away,
As from a dreaded beast of prey,
Before his tread, who scrupled not
To stain with blood the hallowed grot:
But well he knew that half was mine,
To cherish as a holy shrine;
There, prayers ascended morn and even,
A flood of song, to God in heaven!

I walked within the forest shade,
And timid beings round me played :
They did not fear the tread of one,
Who never any harm had done
To them or theirs ; and happy birds
Told me more plainly than by words,
By strains which gushed out wild and clear
Whene'er my wandering steps came near,
Their gratefulness that I had stood
By those who dwell in the green wood.

One day, when I was slowly treading
    Along a valley, fresh and green ;
Light filmy clouds above me spreading,
    With openings of deep blue between ;
Musing upon my stormy life,
With grief and love and passion rife ;
I heard, oh heaven ! can it be true ?
What seemed a distant, faint halloo :
It is, for now upon the breeze
Comes rolling on, through startled trees,
An answering shout, more loud and clear ;
And in the distance did appear
Three, whose loud mirth and manners bold,
Of the wild, changeful ocean told,

With one of different garb and mien :
I saw that yet I was unseen,
And hastened, hardly knowing why,
Into a grove that rose close by,
And stood concealed and trembling there :
It was as I had thought, they were
Upon the search for me, to bear
Me from my solitary home :
And shall I leave this spot, to roam
Again among the heartless crowd,
The mean, the thankless, and the proud?
This beauteous earth! this gorgeous sky!
These waters flowing peacefully!
The joyful morn! the evening time!
The mighty wilderness sublime!
Shall all of these aside be hurled
For the mad music of the world?
But then before me, like a star,
Flashed a bright vision, brighter far
Than all that lavish nature showers
In splendor from her skyey towers :
And with a rapid step and free,
I left the shade exultingly,
And welcomed with a joyful smile,
The strangers to the lonely isle.

16*

Once more upon the ocean tide!
With flashing sail, and mast of pride,
Quivering with life, our vessel bore
Right onward to my native shore;
Dashing the opposing waves apart
With fearless prow, and lordly heart;
Like a besieged and gallant band,
    Breaking through the hostile leaguer,
Scattering with the strong right hand,
    The enclosing ranks of the besieger!
Like a bold, oppressèd nation,
    In a false and faithless age,
Working out its own salvation
    'Mid a stormy sea of rage!

THE RIVALS.

PART III.

Oh Time! great mother of both joy and sorrow!
    Like origin of growth and of decay!
From thy glad bosom springs the sweet to-morrow;
    Within thy lap died tearful yesterday.
The flower of morning in an hour is blighted:
    But, ere the evening, fragrant roses bloom:
Youth sorrows o'er its early promise slighted,
    But bright-eyed Fame soon dissipates the gloom.
The aged die and leave us full of sadness,
    Within our hearts its sable weeds are hung;
The young are born, and fill our souls with gladness,
    And to the breeze joy's sunny folds are flung.
The fierce desires of youth, its stormy passion,
    Like the hot lustre of the bright noonday,
These teachings bless'd of joy and sorrow fashion,
    Until they beam with sunset's holy ray.

Year after year had passed and gone,
Breeze after breeze in swiftness on,
Since I had leaped upon the strand
In triumph of my native land.
The visions of my youth had flown,
And left me doubly now alone.
Yes, like the smooth and silvery sheen
Of waters in the distance seen
By him who wanders faint and weary,
Upon some desert hot and dreary,
They melted into empty air,
And left the calmness of despair.
I cared no more that I had found
None whom I might with joy have bound
Unto my heart of hearts, until
We were one spirit and one will.
No! these were fancies, youthful dreams,
Gay bubbles on funereal streams,
Which flow a while in mist and gloom,
Then sink in earth as in a tomb.

And as my cherished hopes departed,
And left me faithless and cold hearted,
So also faded from my mind
That hatred undeserved and blind,

Which in my better days had spread
Its fatal darkness round my head.
But think not that I loved him more,
Even then, than I had done before;
No! cold indifference had press'd
All but itself from out my breast.
Once only—it was long ago,
Before my heaven had lost its glow,
I wept *his* loss—was it not mine?
For who may claim a thing divine!
He had returned from the lonely isle
To find that death had been busy the while:
The sweet white rose had faded soon;
Dying like a heavenly tune,
Which seemeth not to know decay,
But to slowly pass away;
Like a rosy cloud at even
Melting softly into heaven;
Like a star, when flees the night,
Whitening into liquid light;
Like a flake too pure of birth
To linger long upon the earth!
Yes, as days and months passed by,
And fears gave place to certainty,
Leaf by leaf the white rose fell;
Till one morn a silvery knell

Told that a light and gentle wing
Had sought the realms of endless spring.

Near where I dwelt there was a stream
Which flowed on like a silvery gleam,
Along whose banks I oft would stray
Unmindful of the fleeting day.
Upon each side dark hills arose,
And rocks which threatened to oppose
Its gentle course, but then repenting
Of their harsh purpose, turned relenting,
And left a pathway wide and free
For that young child of liberty!
So wild and lonely was the place,
That none its solemn paths could trace,
And wonder not such scenes should come
So near the city's startling hum.
Alas! its beauties soon will fly;
Dun smoke will shroud its azure sky;
Its giant trees, their gloom sublime,
Like all the gifts of the olden time,
Its hoary rocks, on which is seen
The history of what has been,
Even the dark and primal mountains,
The valleys, and the gushing fountains,

Shall disappear from day to day,
Like useless gifts shall pass away,
For man, with sordid soul and dull,
Reveres no more the beautiful!

One day, when I was wandering through
This lonely vale, where something new
Seems always sure to meet the eye,
Some beauty of the earth or sky
That you have never seen before,
But which then blossoms evermore,
I met a child whose lovely face
Contrasted so with that wild place,
That to my fancy she did seem
Twin sister of the gentle stream.
Her eye, from 'neath its lash of night,
Shone forth at times so purely bright,
That the light of Heaven seem'd streaming through
Its liquid, ever-deepening blue :
Upon her neck dark curls were playing,
Like their sweet owner ever straying
With every breeze that chose to dally
In the cool shade of that wild valley ;
And through her face her soul divine,
As through a cloud the soft moonshine,

Shone with a beauty fairer far
Than the fairest light of the fairest star,
Fairer than aught but the radiant glance
Of its own unveiled countenance.
With courteous tone that fears offence,
And many a vague and weak pretence,
I overcame her diffidence;
And soon we were devoted friends.
That fleeting age was hers, when bends
Above the slender girl a sky
In which she looketh eagerly:
For stars of love are dimly gleaming,
And shapes of beauty haunt her dreaming,
And thrilling tones are faintly heard,
And the deep founts. of life are stirred
By breezy thoughts, that come and go,
Whither alas! she does not know;
And her own spirit is a book
In which she first begins to look,
And finds strange meanings written there,
From which she turns with sad despair,
But soon will come again, and try
To solve the words of destiny;
And solitude begins its reign,
With gentle musings in its train;

And she is full of hope and trust
That all are merciful and just,
And not an hour of life is dull,
But all is quick and wonderful!

Her father's dwelling stood, she said,
Where that slight broken pathway led ;
He was a farmer now, though they
 Once dwelt within the crowded town,—
She liked it not, she could not stray
 As she could here, by dale and down :
" My mother died, alas!" said she,
" When I was in my infancy ;"
And though her sire was very dear,
She wished her mother still were here,
" It were so sweet to have some one
To talk with when the day was done."

Day after day I met the maid ;
Month after month with her I strayed
Along that valley lone and wild,
As would a father with his child.
Oh, it was such delight to see
 The quick unfolding of her powers ;
Like rose-buds opening rapidly
 Beneath alternate sun and showers.
17

She longed for knowledge with a thirst
I could not satisfy at first,
For in each tree, and herb, and sound,
Something mysterious was found:
But for her sake I sought once more
My boyhood's soon-forgotten lore,
Nor deemed that toilsome which could throw
New radiance on her radiant brow.

Sweet Innocent! she little knew,
When, with her wondering eye of blue,
She gazed upon me, as I told
Things always new, and always old,
That she was ever teaching me
In love, and truth, and purity!
Oh! never till before me lay
That breast as open as the day, .
Into whose inmost depths my eye
Might gaze as in a cloudless sky,
Had I perceived the selfishness,
The pride, and anger, and distress,
Which, a chaotic mass, were strewn,
Within the discord of my own.
I am unworthy, thus I said,
        To be beloved by one so bright;

Soon from me will she shrink in dread,
    Like day from the embrace of night,
And leave me desolate, once more,
Upon the wide world's lonely shore.
And then I sought to free my soul
From pride and passion's fierce control,
And banish every sinful thought,
And every wish with evil fraught ;
But soon I sadly found that they
Had taken root from day to day,
Until it seem'd an easier part
To madly pluck up my whole heart, '
Than sever from its native earth,
That which had grown there from my birth.

I tried, and tried, and tried again,
To purify my soul in vain ;
For still unholy thoughts would come
Unto my heart, as to a home ;
And when I hoped that they had vanished,
Forever from my presence banished,
They came again, a wilder band,
And seized the sceptre of command,
And, in a moment, swept away
The fruits of many a watchful day.

At length I could no longer bear
My ill success, and in despair
I wept hot, bitter tears; the first
Which from their fiery wells had burst,
Since, when a miserable child,
I wandered in the lonely wild.
I wept, and then I calmer grew,
'nd dried my tears, and gazed anew
Upon the scene around, which caught
The brightness of a sudden thought :
And on the wave-like ether now,
Which circles from its tuneful prow,
Floats like a vision of the morn,
The melody of a distant horn :
It was a tune I had often heard,
  The tune of a sad, yet joyful lay,
And I knew the ditty every word,
  For 'twas sung by her who had passed away !
It was a tale of an Indian bride,
Who had fallen by her lover's side,
Ere the words of faith were plighted,
Ere the torch of joy was lighted,
Stricken in an instant by
The arrow of Eternity.
For a moment the bridegroom stands,
His dark face quivering 'neath his hands,

Then he kneels, without a tear,
By the side of that maiden dear,
And prays to Him whose word has power
To raise the dead at the judgment hour,
That He will melt with his holy breath
The icy manacles of death,
And give once more to his embrace,
That form of loveliness and grace.
And she woke as from a gentle trance,
And smiles lit up her countenance,
Smiles of joy as she saw her lover
With anxious features bending over.
" Ask of Him, and it shall be given,
  Ask of Him who is ever near ;
Man cannot whisper, but in Heaven
  Pitying spirits bend to hear !"
Thus that soft note seemed to say,
As it slowly died away :
And if, I thought, who reigns above,
Will grant this much to human love ;
If He will touch with quickening power
The early nipped and withered flower,
And make it once again to bloom,
And fling abroad its rich perfume,
Will He not too, restore to me
My childhood's golden purity ?
  17*

And then within my bosom came
An earnest hope I could not name,
I feared to breathe it to the air,
It boldness seemed to call it prayer,
That He would aid me to control
The pride and passion of my soul,
That I might be as pure and mild
And innocent as that dear child.

Day after day we wandered still
Through woods and by the stream at will;
I, minist'ring unto the blind
Though keen desires of her quick mind;
She, teaching me with gentle art,
The holy mysteries of the heart.
And when within my bosom shone
A sinful thought, now there, now gone,
Like the thin, quivering flame which plays
Before the bright and ruddy blaze,
I thought of that sweet Indian ditty,
     And Him who is forever nigh,
Full of power, and full of pity,
     Waiting but the repentant sigh,
And from my heart all passion fled,
And left me calm and quieted.

One morning when with loitering tread
    I wandered through the dewy shade,
Along the winding path which led
    Round craggy rocks, to the smooth glade
    Which we our trysting-place had made,
I heard a sudden scream, and then
A splash, and all was still again.
Trembling with fear, I hurried on
Until the open glade was won,
And dashing through a woody screen,
    I gained the water side, and there
For scarce a moment, saw the sheen
    Of a white hand and forehead fair ;
And must she die, so pure and young!
Fearful I was too late, I sprung
Into the stream, like one who braves
For pearly spoils the ocean caves ;
And soon I saw her, with one hand
    Grasping a water-flower, the other
Beneath her face, while on the sand
    As on the bosom of a mother,
She lay as in a gentle sleep :
It was a sight to make you weep
And smile by turns, to see that she
Could slumber thus, so peacefully !

'Twixt life and death ; and as I bore
Her passive limbs unto the shore,
Her pale hand, with convulsive power,
Still grasped that fragile water flower :
And while she clung to that, I knew
Her spirit to the earth clung too.

With footsteps swift I bore the maid
Through the wild paths, where we had strayed
So gayly but the day before,
Until I reached her father's door ;
And entered in, and on the floor
Laid my sweet burden : then a cry
Of sharp surprise and agony
Burst from the household, but I said,
" Be still ! the maiden is not dead :"
And then the tumult ceased, and all
But two old servants left the hall ;
And they with tears beside her knelt,
    And chafed her snowy limbs, until
The frozen blood did slowly melt,
    And through her veins began to thrill ;
And then I knew she would not die,
And the quick tears came in my eye,
And I thanked him whose word has power
To save ev'n in the darkest hour ;—

And in my soul I heard again
The burden of that Indian strain:
" Ask of God, and it shall be given,
  Ask of Him who is ever near;
Man cannot whisper, but in heaven
  Pitying spirits bend to hear!"
I turned to leave them, but before
My hopeful step had gained the door,
It opened, and the father knelt
By his unconscious child, and felt
Her cold pale cheek, and paler brow,
Which lay beneath his hand like snow;
And then he wept, like one who fears
That naught is left for him but tears.

Oh! as that father wept above
The stricken daughter of his love;
Whom I too loved, with love as wild
As ever parent felt for child;
Our mutual sorrow seemed to be
A bond of peace and sympathy.
What though I once had shrunk away
  From him who now before me stood;
I had grown wiser since that day,
  Through her, the innocent and good!

And in his features I could trace
Some slight resemblance to her face.
A moment—and I stood beside
The maid, and cheerfully replied
Unto his sad, desponding look,
" She will not die !" and then he took
My hands in his, and faltering told,
With thanks that would not be controlled,
His joy that I was near to save
His only daughter from the grave.

Week after week the maiden lay,
And knew no change from day to day;
We watched by turns, her sire and I,
 By her low bed from hour to hour ;
Forgotten was our enmity :
 Love, with its stronger, holier power,
Had driven out the fiend of hate :
We thought not of our former state ;
We only thought of her who still
Lay waiting the eternal will ;
And when the light of life again
Broke like a pure, bewitching strain,
From her sweet face, and on her tongue
Soft tones of joy enraptured hung,

As if unwilling to depart
From their harmonious home, her heart,
Our mutual joy was a stronger tie
Of love, which springs from sympathy,
Than even our mutual grief had been:
And we would oft together then
Sit by the bed of that fair girl,
And smiles would light her cheek of pearl,
As she in playful thought would speak
Of her two fathers.

      · Thus the bleak
And weary winter of my life,
  Was melted by the breath of spring;
And from the elemental strife,
  Came beauty and sweet blossoming!

THE END.

www.ingramcontent.com/pod-product-compliance
Lightning Source LLC
Chambersburg PA
CBHW030829020726
47499CB00006B/2134